UNDER THE CHAMPAGNE MOON

ALINA K. FIELD

HAVENLOCK PRESS

Cover Design by Dar Albert of Wicked Smart Designs

Under the Champagne Moon

Orphaned by the French Revolution and rescued by a British family, Fleur Hardouin was a solemn and often sullen child. She didn't—or wouldn't—speak, until the jolly young Gareth Ardleigh crossed her path one summer and saved her from bullies.

Fifteen years later, Fleur's life takes another twist when she and the beloved lady she serves lose their home and return to the town of Reabridge. Determined to rescue them both through an advantageous marriage, Fleur tries to brush off the attention she receives from Captain Gareth Ardleigh, who's home from the wars and as handsome as ever. Her heart longs for him, but her head knows he can't provide the security she needs.

Gareth's excuse for visiting Reabridge is to deliver the personal effects of his best friend who perished at Quatre Bras. But his real purpose is finding the little French girl he met years ago, for marriage—not to him, but to the Frenchman who helped save his life. Little does Fleur know that she's heir to a wealthy French vintner who's demanded Gareth's help finding Fleur as repayment of his rescue from Napoleon's army.

Astonished to find that Fleur has grown into a beautiful—and still intriguing—young woman, it soon becomes clear, he must choose between honoring a promise or trying to win the hand of the woman he loves.

Previously published in *Under the Harvest Moon, a Bluestocking Belles Collection with Friends*

CHAPTER ONE

SUMMER, 1800

CHESHIRE, ENGLAND

On this glorious summer's day, Gareth Ardleigh reveled in the riches of Sherington Manor. Fish begging to be caught, small game fattened by summer's bounty, and trees promising climbers wide vistas. He and his school friends, Thaddeus and Laurence Sherington, skirted the edge of the park, guns and rabbits in hand when they came upon an altercation. Two boys and a girl loomed over a thin little waif with hair so pale it was almost white.

"Say summat in French," the bullying girl lisped.

Limp hair straggled over dirty cheeks to a lank, dingy pinafore, drawing the eye down to bare brown feet.

In fact, only the biggest bully wore footwear—scuffed, holey boots at least one size two big.

"She can't," the shorter boy sneered, leaning in on his quarry. "As dumb as that tree over there, she is."

Inside the circle of dirty, ill-dressed tormentors, the specter bristled, her brows drawn together in a defiant glare that was bigger than her small self.

"That's Flora," Thaddeus said. "She lives at Bicton Grange."

"She doesn't speak," Laurence said. "That other lot are the Haskells, up from lower Reabridge to help with the haying."

"Croak for us, Froggie." The big Haskell stepped closer and the other two sniggered.

The one thing Gareth couldn't abide was bullies. He handed Laurence his gun, dropped his game, and winked at Thaddeus.

He and Thad had battled their way through Rugby School together, and neither would back away from a fight.

"Leave off." Gareth snatched the ringleader's shirt and yanked him back. Cloth ripped, and three shocked faces turned his way.

Their shock turned to anger, followed by a fist. Gareth ducked, and Thaddeus flew into the fray, taking on the shorter boy.

"Stop it," their sister squawked, and then shrieked. When Gareth spared a glance, the dirty chit had curled up on the ground, spluttering curses, while her would-be victim kicked at her.

He laughed and tossed the ringleader down. "Get you gone, all three of you. If I see you bullying again, I'll do more than bloody your noses."

"She's a bluidy French—"

"Watch your mouth." Thad slapped the younger lad.

"Take the king's shilling and join up if you want to fight," Gareth said. It was what he and Thad were doing at summer's end. "But don't pick on babies."

The baby in question glared at him, and while he swallowed a chuckle, all three Haskells tucked tail and ran.

Thaddeus clapped Gareth on the back, laughing. "Bang up to the mark, Gare," he said. "You planted a solid facer. Looks like he clipped you one though." He tapped Gareth's chin and held up a bloody finger.

Gareth touched the wound. "So he did." Laughing, he dabbed at it with his neck cloth.

"Use a handkerchief, man," Laurence scoffed.

"Don't have one." Gareth's gaze caught the imp watching him. There was no look of gratitude at their chivalry. She still glared.

He felt a stab of—well, not guilt. Recognition— that was it. His name-calling had wounded her pride.

The best remedy for wounded pride was the schoolboy's solution—a good fight. Perhaps with enough goading, she'd kick him.

"Are you alone?" he asked. "Where is your nursemaid? Ought we to take you home?"

"Oh, she's alright," Laurence said. "Move out of our way, Flora." He nudged her aside and he and Thaddeus walked on.

Gareth studied the chit while she stared back, her gaze far too steady for one so young. She couldn't be more than five or six with the palest of hair, the lightest of gray eyes, and skin as white as a ghost's, all wrapped in a white gown. Aside from a fringe of mud on her hem, a touch of light brown in her eyebrows and lashes, and some pink in her lips, the scrawny young stick had no more color in her than a skinned rabbit. His scrutiny wasn't even raising a blush.

"Flora?" he said in the same teasing tone he applied to his infant cousins. And most other people as well, come to think of it. "You ought to be called Daisy, or Daffy."

The pink bow of her lips thinned.

"Or," he snapped his fingers, "Petal. Just Petal. I shall call you that."

She drew her tiny self up, as haughty as Headmaster Ingles before he took out his strop. "My name," she said in perfectly accented English, "is Fleur."

Fleur? Flora, Daisy, Daffy, Petal... but Fleur? The ridiculousness of it made him laugh as he picked up his gun and rabbits and ran to catch up with his friends.

Thereafter, Petal seemed to appear everywhere he and Thaddeus went fishing, hunting, tree-climbing. She'd even attended the end of summer picnic at Sherington Manor with her guardian, still not speaking, except in the frowns and grimaces she showered upon him when he called her Petal.

The day he departed for a visit home to farewell his family before joining the regiment and taking up his ensign duties, he made one last walk savoring the peace he'd found at Sherington Manor. The little chit tracked him down and handed him a square of white cloth.

It was a man's handkerchief; golden petals straggled around the edges in clumsy, uneven stitches.

A handkerchief. His new messmates in the regiment would think he had an amour. Would he look like a fool if they knew this came from a mere baby?

A laugh bubbled up and spilled over. Despite himself, he was touched. But when he looked up to thank her, she'd disappeared.

* * *

SEPTEMBER, *1815*

ON A BRISK EARLY AUTUMN MORNING THE DAY AFTER his arrival in Cheshire, Captain Gareth Ardleigh rode past fields swarming with laborers harvesting corn. Back-breaking labor it was, as he well knew from his days growing up on his gentry father's modest estate. In bad years or good—especially in good—gentleman or not, all hands were needed. Returning to school for the Michaelmas term had always been a blessed reprieve, and he'd made good friends there, Thaddeus Sherington and to a lesser degree Thad's older brother Laurence. Gareth had been warmly welcomed for visits by George Sherington and his lady wife. Those had been good times. Sadly, Mrs. Sherington died a little over a year ago. And Thad...

He reined up and gazed down the long drive to Bicton Grange, a square stone manse with a filled in moat and overgrown hedges. Tall grass had overtaken the lawns too, except where wheel tracks carved crescents around a crater-sized hole in the bumpy lane.

The Bicton-Morledge family had fallen on hard times. It was unfortunate, but not something he could help with. He had a small—very small— income from his late uncle, and somehow, he would live on it. His elder brother had not demanded

Gareth's return to the family fold; had been grateful, in fact, for one less mouth to feed.

He'd come to Reabridge first to visit the Sheringtons, and then... Well, once he finished here, if roaming around the country as an officer on half pay became boring, he could return to active duty and risk dying of a fever in either the East or the West Indies. He was, at least, alive now, as Thaddeus wasn't, having fallen, finally, after so many battles, at Quatre Bras.

Laurence might be an annoying complainer, but he'd accepted Thad's personal effects with almost as much grief as his mournful father and his watery-eyed widowed cousin, Mrs. Esther Smythe, who served as the Sherington chatelaine since Mrs. Sherington's passing. They'd invited Gareth to stay on through the harvest, and longer, if he wished.

Which served Gareth's needs quite well. For, much as he was honored to perform the task, delivering Thad's things wasn't his only reason for visiting Reabridge. He had a debt to repay, and to do so, he must find a female whom he'd last seen here.

He'd start looking in earnest tomorrow. Today, he'd ride back to Sherington Manor and open another bottle of champagne.

* * *

"MR. SHERINGTON WON'T HAVE YOU, GEL. I'LL WAGER you a quid on that."

Fleur Hardouin sent the snowy-haired lady next to her a haughty look. Lady Dulcinea Ixworth, the granddaughter of a duke and widow of a long-deceased viscount, perched perilously on the seat as Fleur handled the lines, making no move to clutch the siderail of Bicton Grange's rickety gig. Dulcinea was, as usual, fearless, and full of vinegar.

"If either of us had a quid to spare, madame," Fleur said, "I would take that wager."

She suspected she might lose, of course, but that would be fine. No one in her life had been more generous than Dulcinea Ixworth in sharing small bounties.

"Perhaps he won't see us, as ill as he's been," Dulcinea said, pressing her lips together.

Fleur glanced at her companion. Fearless Dulcinea might be, but Fleur sensed a heightened tension in her employer. Dulcinea had donned her newest gown, lavender half-mourning trimmed in intricate silver embroidery at the neckline and hem by Fleur's own skilled hands. With her carefully coifed hair and newly trimmed bonnet, Dulcinea looked magnificent for this call on an old acquaintance.

Providing that Mr. George Sherington was able to receive them. Just months earlier, the fever that had taken Mr. Bicton-Morledge to the grave had struck Mr. Sherington. Mrs. Knollwood, the housekeeper at Bicton Grange, who'd been a beloved housemaid when Fleur was a child there, had learned that the local doctor said Mr. Sherington ought to have come out of his Bath chair weeks ago.

The doctor apparently had returned from Waterloo with a penchant for drink that sometimes loosened his tongue too much.

"The son will be more likely for you," Dulcinea said, interrupting Fleur's revery.

"But not more manageable." Fleur urged the horse onto the lane leading to Sherington Manor. While one son had gone off to the army, Laurence had been home for school holidays, and she remembered him well. Unless he'd changed, he'd be bossy and careless of a wife. One could tolerate a bossy man for a few years, but Laurence would likely live another thirty.

She glanced at the small smile turning up her employer's rouged lips. "I would have liked one more day of rest after our journey, but I suppose we must strike while the iron is hot. Today Sherington Manor and tomorrow—"

"Yes, yes." Interrupting was rude, but Fleur's nerves were on edge. She'd never pursued matrimony before. "Since this visit to Reabridge was your idea in the first place, madame."

Dulcinea snorted, something she only did in private with Fleur. "Rife with prosperous older men, it is. A better hunting ground for you, gel than any other place we might have chosen."

Or been able to afford.

It would at least be a new one. Ten years before, she'd left Reabridge, naught but a scrawny girl of twelve, cast off by her frustrated guardian to serve as the companion of an aging relation who lived with a scholarly cousin in Staffordshire.

She'd grown to be a woman there, one not allowed to indulge in sulking. From the very first day, Dulcinea had poked, prodded, and even laughed at her silent stubbornness. Until the damn broke and Fleur talked, shouted, screamed back.

Dulcinea had allowed it. She'd listened. She'd drawn out the hurts, the resentments, the sadness. She'd made Fleur talk. She'd paid attention, pushed her to learn from books and intelligent conversations, taught her to manage a household.

As Fleur reached womanhood, Dulcinea shared more—naughty stories from her youth, lessons about men, about how to deflect the unsavory suitors an attractive young woman with no dowry or male relative might expect.

Dulcinea had saved her.

They'd reached Bicton Grange the previous evening, a *visit* arranged by Dulcinea, fortuitously since the two of them had just been put out of their prior home by the death of Basil Quidenham,

Dulcinea's cousin. Such were the vicissitudes of fate for widows and orphans.

It had, however, been clear upon their arrival that Mrs. Helena Bicton-Morledge positively needed them. She'd aged considerably in the years since Fleur last saw her, and was now immensely with child—twins, Mrs. Knollwood suspected. Plus, the Bicton-Morledge girls, three misses ranging from sixteen to four years of age, were running amuck, and the remaining servants were stretched thin.

Fleur would take the young chits and the household in hand this very day, as soon as she'd begun this campaign to see to her own future.

TWENTY MINUTES LATER, SHE EXCUSED HERSELF FROM the stiff settee and the overly warm drawing room of Sherington Manor where their hostess, Mrs. Smythe, poured tea and made excuses for the Sherington men. Neither of the Sheringtons was at home for the ladies, but the cousin was more than happy to have the likes of Lady Ixworth, the granddaughter of a duke, visiting.

While Dulcinea probed Mrs. Smythe about Sherington's health, Fleur decided to act. She waved off the offer of a guiding hand to the retiring room. She'd visited Sherington Manor on one or two occasions as a child and knew where to find the water closet.

Her quest, however, was the location of the male voices echoing from another part of the house. Laurence would be there, maybe with his steward discussing the harvest, and perhaps even his father would be present. The men must be in high spirits for their voices to carry all the way to the drawing room, and wasn't that interesting? They were probably happy to pawn their guests off on their middle-aged cousin.

She arrived at a paneled door that fairly quivered with masculine vibrations. As her hand touched the knob, a man's laugh made her pause. She pressed her ear to the painted wood.

CHAPTER TWO

"*I* will show you the art of sabrage, Laurence. Only but watch my technique."

A shiver passed through her, followed by heat that turned her hands and cheeks clammy. The voice, the cocky intonation... She paused, gathered her composure, and then turned the knob.

The door opened on silent hinges, cigar smoke wafting to meet her. Silver flashed. An object shot out and bounced against the fireplace shovel with a loud bang, and the air bubbled with the scent of fermented grapes.

A well-dressed gentleman sat behind a heavy desk, cigar in hand. The other, his curly dark locks in disarray, coatless, and with very fine legs encased in tight buckskins, stood before the desk, his back to the door.

"Dans la victoire," the man in buckskins proclaimed, *"tu mérites du champagne, et dans la défaite tu en as besoin."*

In victory you deserve champagne, and in defeat you need it?

Her stomach twisted, thoughts stirring in her muddled mind. It had sounded like *him*, but it couldn't be, could it? Nor was it Thaddeus—he'd fallen at Waterloo.

Had *he* lived?

If it wasn't *him*...would Sherington be hosting a blasted *Frenchman?*

Laurence—surely the weak-chinned blond fellow behind the desk *was* Laurence—noticed her. Thaddeus had been the handsomer of the two boys. Poor Thaddeus.

Laurence's smile fell away as he stood and set aside his cigar. The man with him, the man clutching a foaming bottle in one hand and a saber in the other, turned his head. His lips widened and softened, and his eyes darkened with what she recognized as a man's carnal interest.

And then they widened with shock. A smile dawned, flooding his face with something that looked like relief.

Her own heart thundered. *Gareth.* This *was* Gareth, grown into a man, with thighs that would send Dulcinea into embarrassing public ecstasies.

"Petal," he cried. "It's *you.*"

"Flora?" Laurence stepped closer, his gaze traveling over her like an annoying insect buzzing around. "I haven't seen you in years. Is it *really* you? All grown up?"

The tone was lascivious and didn't deserve a reply.

Laurence rounded the desk and scoffed. "Don't tell me you still don't speak, Flora."

That again. The fool.

"*My name*," she said, "is Fleur. Not Flora. Nor is it Petal."

Gareth's eyes twinkled, flecks of gold sparking among the brown, and his whole face lit from within as if he was holding in one of his hearty laughs, like the one that exploded out of him the last time she saw him.

Did he still have the handkerchief she'd labored over? He'd probably thrown it into the fire the same day he'd received it.

And that was fine. Gareth had no place in her plans.

"Welcome back from the wars, Ardleigh." Broad shouldered and narrow waisted, his only visible scar traced one jawline. Were there others? *She'd* never know. "I see you're in blessedly good health. But Mr. Sherington, may I offer my condolences to you on your brother's death? I'm sorry for your loss."

Laurence dipped his head, and a cloud passed over Gareth's face, ever so briefly.

He hadn't changed. Nothing could shake him out of his native good humor for long. "You may both address me as Miss Hardouin," she said. "Do please come along to the drawing room, Mr. Sherington and be introduced to Lady Dulcinea Ixworth. She is most anxious to meet you, and to renew her acquaintance with your father. Might you persuade him to join us?"

* * *

GARETH ALLOWED HIMSELF A SMILE AT HER BOLDNESS, Laurence's gaping mouth, and the fact that she hadn't included Gareth in the commanding invitation. Fleur was as much a pert little baggage as ever, more so now that she was a gabby one, and she'd grown in all the best ways, from the golden curls peeking from under her bonnet to the trim ankles under her too-short skirts. And all the curves in between.

Especially those.

If Thad were here to see how the skinny little chit had grown…

But he wasn't, dammit. Gareth had been the lucky one, in battle, in his rescue, even in his case of the precious Vin de Comête.

And now this: Fleur Hardouin was right here. His search was over. He could send a letter to Etienne Marceau telling the Frenchman he'd found him his bride, and then be free to be on his own way.

"Beg pardon, Miss, er Hardouin," Laurence said, interrupting his thoughts, "but Ardleigh and I are—"

"Oh, why don't we join the ladies, Laurence?" Gad, she was lovely, and he wanted to know more about her. He had to make sure she was the right Mademoiselle Hardouin, didn't he? Not that there was any doubt—she looked astonishingly like the miniature of her mother. "That is, if I'm included in the invitation."

Fleur waved a regal hand. "Do bring the champagne," she said. "It is a particular favorite of my lady when she can get it."

He chuckled. "Is it indeed? Then I shall look forward to hearing her opinion on the vintage." This particular bottle was not the Vin de Comête. He'd smuggled in a case of the coveted 1811 vintage champagne, a hedge against poverty in the unknowable future. Putting aside his saber, he grasped the bottle in one hand and set his other lightly to her elbow, inhaling the delicate scent of floral perfume. Not lavender—his old nurse had reeked of the stuff. Not roses either.

He dipped his head her way and sniffed. "*Mmm. Lilac?*"

Her eyes turned a steely gray, and the slight wash of color creeping up her pale neck cheered him beyond reason. Fleur was a flower, but not a fragile one, and not one to blush easily at an importuning man's flattery.

Or... he suspected that the cynical young girl had not grown into that sort of woman. What did he really know of her in the years since he'd last seen her?

She was still a Miss Hardouin, so she hadn't married.

"Come along." True to form, she quick-marched out of the library with him tagging along attached to her arm.

"Who is this Lady Dulcinea Ixworth?" he asked.

She sent him a side-wise condescending look, the sort you'd bestow on a child who'd asked a stupid question.

Another grin tugged at his lips, and he swallowed a laugh. He'd always enjoyed young Petal's silent testiness, but in Fleur the woman? The challenge was as intoxicating as champagne.

A new thought nagged: would Etienne Marceau appreciate her?

"She's a distant cousin to the Bicton-Morledges." Fleur's frosty tone pull him out of his reverie. "I've been serving as her hired companion."

"Does she live at Bicton Grange?"

"No. Well, that is, we only just arrived from Staffordshire."

"Staffordshire."

"Yes."

"How did you come to..." He thought of the sulking little girl Fleur used to be. "Do you mean that Bicton-Morledge sent you away?"

Fleur tugged her arm free and turned on him. "Think you that Mr. Bicton-Morledge and his lady would cast off an orphan?"

He passed by the ravaged drive and unkempt park at Bicton Grange. Perhaps clothing and feeding Fleur had been too much of a burden. But surely Fleur had some money from her parents.

He'd learned some of her history from his time spent in France. If she was, in fact, the right Miss Hardouin—and how could she not be?—her father had been a son of a crafty textile and wine merchant. While Fleur's grandfather changed sides as needed during the revolution, Fleur's father opposed the sans culottes, and then, perforce, was disowned by his family. He'd joined the counterrevolution and been executed in Lyon when Fleur was no more than an infant.

Gareth had seen a miniature of Fleur's mother, a blond and strikingly beautiful daughter of a minor *seigneur*. All of that family had been lost to the ravaging peasants. Perhaps there truly had been no money following young Fleur to Switzerland when she and her mother escaped.

Unless the late Bicton-Morledge had squandered his young ward's inheritance. Always a possibility.

Fleur still watched him, a glint in her eyes that was not humor.

He touched her elbow again. "Perhaps they were tired of your long silences."

Her shoulders rose and fell in a huff, and she continued down the corridor.

He ought to apologize, but this was Fleur, and she'd never been a child to appreciate insincere coddling. As a woman—well, time would tell, but he doubted she'd developed a taste for polite lies.

"How long have you served the lady?" he asked.

"Ten years."

"*Ten years*? You couldn't have been more than—"

"I was twelve when I came to her."

Sent off as a child to serve as a companion? Why? What had his Petal done to deserve that fate?

Their arrival at the drawing room door silenced his questions, and he stepped aside to let Fleur enter first, watching the sway of her hips and the delicate slope of her shoulders under her gown.

Serving as drudge to an older lady hadn't dampened her pride or her spirits. Yet what an awful life, fetching shawls, brewing possets, and who knew what other more disagreeable tasks were required.

The marriage to Marceau planned by her grandmother, the Veuve Hardouin would save her from that life. She'd have her own home, wouldn't she? Or would she and Marceau be required to live under the thumb of the Veuve?

Mrs. Smythe sat near the fire, an elegant older lady nearby. Curls as white as his neck cloth burst from under the visitor's bonnet. The lady wore lavender, as did Fleur. Half-mourning? For Bicton-Morledge or someone else?

"Good day to you, ladies." Gareth bestowed his most charming smile.

He watched as Fleur's back stiffened, suppressing a chuckle. Her hair had darkened over the years, and the coil of regal gold sparkled under the back of her tiny bonnet. By God, Fleur ought to be a royal princess instead of a princess of the champagne world.

Sherington's Cousin Esther looked up, relief easing her tense mouth. A timid, compliant widow who'd needed a home, she'd been happy to take on hostess duties when Sherington lost his wife a year earlier.

The older guest raised a quizzing glass to her eyes, and he felt that bright, magnified eyeball creeping from the top of his head to the tip of his boots. And then up again pausing over-long at his unmentionables.

He smiled and raised the bottle of champagne in a salute.

"Dulcinea? Is it really you?"

The gravelly voice behind him caught him by surprise. He'd missed the creaking of Laurence's father's Bath chair rolling behind him.

"Indeed, Sherington." The lady's mellifluous voice had none of the raspiness of aging. "What's the meaning of you gadding about in a chair with wheels? Are there no good chairmen in Cheshire to carry you about the house?"

George Sherington laughed long and heartily.

"Father?" Laurence sent Gareth a curious glance at this rare display of good spirits. Sherington's illness had taken him down, Laurence said, but even before that he'd been grieving dreadfully since his wife's death. The losses that followed, of his friend, Bicton-Morledge, and worst of all, Thaddeus, had been heavy blows.

Sherington's man wheeled him closer to the ladies and helped him transfer to the settee where the visiting lady sat.

Laurence sent a servant to fetch champagne glasses, and then introductions were made. Lady Ixworth extended a slim regal hand while her gaze skipped over Laurence and settled on Gareth again with a glittery interest that would have put a Covent Garden dove to shame. He swallowed the urge to laugh.

Fleur surely noticed the older lady's interest. Her lips and eyes squeezed shut for the briefest of moments. Was she embarrassed?

When she cleared her throat and spoke, she told Laurence's father how wonderful it was to see him after so many years.

Fleur, transformed, as genteel as a Mayfair maiden or her mother.

He chuckled. What was she up to?

Mr. Sherington looked just as perplexed, but he was quickly distracted by Lady Ixworth, who peppered him with the sort of teasing that signaled more than a mere acquaintance. Gad, as if they'd once been much, *much* more than mere acquaintances.

What an entertaining visit this was proving to be.

When the glasses had been filled and passed around, Fleur pulled a chair next to old Sherington, listening as if captivated.

Perhaps Lady Ixworth's health was failing, and Fleur was fishing for a position as Sherington's nurse.

Unless she thought being kind to the father might hook her Laurence's hand?

No. She couldn't marry Laurence. She was to marry Marceau, though she didn't know it, and Marceau didn't deserve her, and wouldn't know how to handle a girl like her.

Fleur carried the mercenary blood of the Veuve Hardouin, a woman who had wriggled her way through the revolutionary madness and charmed Bonaparte with sparkling wine. Marceau was a mere watered-down distant cousin. No proper match for Fleur.

And yet... he needed to tell Fleur he'd discovered

her family. Not here, though, and not now in front of an audience.

* * *

The next day

Fleur settled a breakfast tray on the table in Mrs. Bicton-Morledge's bedchamber while sixteen-year-old Cora helped her mother from the bed.

"So kind of you to help, Fleur," the lady called, struggling to sit up. Her white linen nightgown flowed like stout canvas tenting a heavy boulder. Cora knelt before her mama and helped her into her slippers. "If only I could see my feet. Thank you, my darling girl."

A pretty, petite lass, Cora was the image of what her mother must have looked like at that age, with dark curling hair and deep blue eyes. She was the eldest of the three Bicton-Morledge girls; that is, the eldest at home. Phyllis, who must now be nineteen, had run off with a soldier three years prior. The son of the family had died tragically in a fall from a horse. The two younger girls, Jemimah, aged eight and Suze, aged four, were in the nursery with one of the few remaining servants, a devoted nursery maid.

Cora helped her mother through her ablutions while a maid popped in to carry out the night waste, and they soon had the lady settled more or less comfortably into a chair.

Fleur drew the table closer and lifted the covers revealing shirred eggs, ham, and buttered toast.

"Heavens, how am I to eat so much?"

"Try, ma'am," Fleur said.

Cora tucked a napkin over her mother's expansive lap and dove for it when it slid to the floor. "Tuck this into your bodice, Mama, and eat. Cook says you must keep up your strength."

The lady grasped her daughter's hand and smiled. "Are you gossiping about me with the servants?"

Fleur's heart twisted. Mrs. Bicton-Morledge had been a distant, almost cold guardian to her younger self, and perhaps it had been in part her own fault. The lady had just lost one child and had another on the way when the family took in Fleur. Having a surly young girl thrust into her care must have bewildered her.

Cora dropped a kiss on her mother's cheek. "It's only that we care about you. All of us."

Fleur turned away from the tender scene and took a step toward the door.

"Wait, Fleur," the lady said. "Thank you, Cora. Now, will you run along and see to your sisters? I want to speak with Fleur a moment."

CHAPTER THREE

*D*read threaded through her. Surely the lady wouldn't send them away, not yet anyway.

"Come pull that chair closer." Mrs. Bicton-Morledge beckoned her. "Would you like some of this toast? I couldn't possibly eat all of it."

"No, thank you, ma'am." Fleur drew a chair a fraction closer and smoothed the skirts of her lavender kerseymere gown under the white smock she'd borrowed from Mrs. Knollwood.

"You left here as a child, but you've come back as a lady. I think you must call me Helena. Will you do that?"

Stunned, Fleur almost refrained from speaking. But perhaps she'd done too much of that in the past. Mrs. Bic... Helena, did not deserve any more defiant silence. "Why... yes. Yes, I will."

Helena grimaced. "It is better than the Mrs. Bicton-Morledge mouthful. Now why are you wearing that smock? You're not a servant."

"Dulcinea—Lady Ixworth—and I, we're grateful you took us in. And we mean to help you in any way we may."

There. It had been said.

The lady's dimpled hand reached for hers. "I'm so happy to see the person you've become. I've been troubled all these years about not doing more for you as a child. About sending you away. There. I've said it."

Fleur let out a breath, marveling at the echoed sentiment, and her heart lifted.

Helena squeezed Fleur's hand. "Do you remember..." She took in a breath and started again. "I wanted to tell you what I could of your mother, but my husband felt it would make your... your troubled state worse. And then as you got older... I hoped we might visit you or you might visit us and I could tell you in person, rather than putting it into a letter."

Heart pounding, Fleur nodded. "I am here now, Mrs., er, Helena."

"Yes. I won't die knowing I ought to have told you this. Do you remember anything of the time before you came to us?"

Fleur straightened in her chair. Sometimes an image would flash, cloudy, dream-like, a woman with hair like her own, and soft. But crying, always crying. And another, dark-haired—though she couldn't put a face to either of them. Often, a strong whiff of jasmine would unsettle the fog, though never enough. Was that why she favored the scent?

She must find out what Helena knew. "No," she said.

"A Swiss woman who worked as a modiste brought you to my husband. She told him what she knew of your parents, their names, where they were from, and where you born, and he wrote it down. He did give you that, didn't he?"

Fleur nodded. She'd always known her parents' names, but the brief account had been among the legal papers she'd received when she'd reached her majority the year before.

"Your mother had sewed for the modiste, but... she died, and apparently, they found you crying beside her body. We were packing to leave—oh there was such chaos, with uprisings and the French army advancing. My husband brought you home, and we took you with us. No one dreamed the war would last this long, but now that it's surely over, perhaps you'd like to see what remains of your family?"

A familiar flash of anger warmed her face. As if her meager funds would support such a quest.

And what an ungrateful thought. Though she didn't have much, Mr. Bicton-Morledge had arranged a small income for her before his own family fortunes declined.

"Lady Ixton is my family now," she said.

Helena squeezed her hand again. "As are we, my girls and I." A frown creased her brow. "Dulcinea mentioned your wish to find some security through marriage. When the time comes, you must make certain of a proper settlement, a dower and a promise to provide for children. And if there is an entail..."

Ah, yes. Bicton Grange was entailed. Helena and her girls were perilously close to being homeless.

"You mustn't worry," Fleur said. "Dulcinea and I, between us, have enough income for a roof over our heads, and yours, and your girls' as well." It would be a tiny roof, but they'd have shelter. "Dulcinea will delight in bossing the little girls and you while you recover from childbirth. You are going to be just fine."

If need be, she'd pour coffee down the village doctor's throat to sober him, be sure of that.

"Nevertheless..." Helena took in a shallow breath. "Oh heavens, I can barely breathe with this girl kicking me. You are kind, Fleur. And should I not make it—"

"You will."

"But should I not, it does my heart good to hear you say you'll help my girls. I fear my husband's cousin will be as ungenerous as Dulcinea's cousin's heir." She shuddered. "Jedidiah Morledge pounds his bible prodigiously, but when he came for my dear husband's funeral... He insisted on speaking to the doctor about my condition. Mr. Sherington hadn't yet fallen ill, and it took his intervention—acting as Justice of the Peace and guardian to my girls—as well as that of our solicitor who'd come down from Manchester, to convince Jedidiah he must wait until this child is born to claim ownership and evict us." Helena's hand shook around her teacup. "Poor, dear, Sherington. We almost lost him, too. What would I have done?"

"Mr. Sherington seems to have rallied," Fleur said.

"Thank goodness. Now, we must not worry, my girls won't be entirely penniless either after their new sister arrives. And I know Sherington and our solicitor won't fail them. My dear, don't let your concern for them keep you from marrying."

"Why, Helena," Fleur said, "that wee one kicking you might be a boy. And you've borne five healthy children before; you will come through beautifully, providing you keep your strength up. Please do eat, or Cook will fret."

"Cook will always fret. I believe I must bestir myself and attempt to go downstairs for dinner tonight, if only to keep her from leaving us like the butler did."

Fleur stood. If the worst should happen, the very worst, she'd write the Bicton-Morledge girls into any marriage agreement she made. A husband who wouldn't help care for orphans was no man at all, at least not a man to suit her.

"Don't go just yet," Helena said. "I want to discuss the plans for the Harvest Festival. I intend for Bicton Grange to participate as we always do with biscuits and cakes for the parish booth, and the girls will take part in the fun. Cora *must* attend the ball that night— she has an admirer in Mr. Haskell, you know. And then," she squeezed Fleur's hand, "let us review the list of available bachelors for you in Reabridge."

* * *

IT WAS AFTER NOON WHEN FLEUR FOUND DULCINEA settled into a chair by the waning fire in her bedchamber. "And where have you been, gel? I had to wait for the kitchen maid to carry away my dishes."

With her back turned, Fleur rolled her eyes, and fetched an extra shawl from the bed. Dulcinea had been in to chat with Helena after Fleur left, so she knew perfectly well Fleur had visited the nursery, helped in the still room, and accompanied the lone footman, James, delivering the harvest crews' meat pies, another tradition that Bicton Grange would keep up. The harvest had begun in earnest, and she would be lucky if she wasn't asked to grab a pitchfork and help.

And that would be alright. The talk with Helena that morning had unsettled her. Keeping busy meant she didn't have to think.

Avoiding Dulcinea's bright gaze, she settled the colorful cloth over the older lady's legs and went to poke at the fire.

"Hah. Squash your lips together like that, gel, they'll stay that way permanently and no man will want to kiss you."

If she kept to her plan and captured an old man, not being kissed would be just fine.

"Not speaking, are you? You said little enough at the Sheringtons'."

That was a lie. She'd been all that was polite toward old Mr. Sherington. It was Laurence and Gareth she'd ignored.

Dulcinea twirled her quizzing glass. "You'll not win Sherington by mere fussing, you know. He always fancied the gels with some spark. When he was younger… What a man. What thighs." She shivered. "That horse-faced son must take after his mother. But the other fellow, Ardleigh made me wish I was forty years younger." She laughed. "Or twenty years. After Ixworth died, a young man with fine legs like his—"

"Yes, yes," Fleur said. "You ought to have turned

your flirting on Ardleigh and given me more of a chance with Mr. George Sherington."

"Softening him up for you, is all. He and I..." She sighed and a dreamy look came over her. "There was a ball, oh some thirty years ago—"

"Oh, do spare me the talk of your conquests, my lady," she teased. Dulcinea had been a beauty in her youth, and she was still quite comely, with a trim figure and skin she'd guarded well from the sun. "Shall you set your cap for him, then?"

"Heavens, no. Play nursemaid to an old goat in his dotage? In a Bath chair? No, no, he'd have to break that up for kindling." She glanced toward the cheery flames, her lips quivering into a small smile. "Though there was a time when he was like a prime stallion. Times were different then."

"Perhaps you can, er, revive him," Fleur said. "He clearly favored you over me. Mrs. Bicton-Morledge has promised to help me meet Miss Farnham, whose widowed father is sure to be nearby." Miss Farnham kept house for her father on a very fine manor in lower Reabridge. The presence of the spinster daughter might pose an obstacle to matrimony, but Fleur wasn't greedy. If he would but provide a small cottage for Dulcinea, she would do her duty by everyone and when the time came, would settle for a small income upon Mr. Farnham's passing. All else might go to the daughter.

"Will you come along on this call?" Fleur asked.

"And if young Sherington and his friend call tomorrow?"

"There is no guarantee they'll call, and I must be about the business of securing the future."

"With an old man." Dulcinea shook her head. "It is a good plan, sensible, and yet I cannot truly like it for a spirited girl like you. Are you sure this will answer? There was a spark in Ardleigh's eyes when he looked at you."

"Ah yes, the spark. You've always told me to beware the spark." She bit her lips to keep from smiling. "Ardleigh is a younger son, and likely has no income, or next to none."

Dulcinea harrumphed.

The sound of a carriage on the drive drew Fleur to the window. A landau had drawn up. Gareth jumped out and turned to help another man who leaned heavily on his arm, a cane bracing him on the other side.

"Who is it?"

Fleur hurried to the clothes press. "Sherington is here. We must get you dressed."

"Pah" Dulcinea flapped a hand. "You go visit him. What a pity he didn't bring his friend Ardleigh."

Fleur whisked away the lap blanket. "Oh, Ardleigh has come along as well. And the Sherington with him is George." She smiled. "And he's walking."

Dulcinea's eyes glinted. In fact, they positively

sparked. "Is that so? Well come along, gel. Don't stand there dawdling."

A FEW MINUTES LATER, MRS. KNOLLWOOD CAUGHT them in the corridor, winded from hurrying up the stairs.

"Oh, miss, my lady, before you go down..." She paused for a breath. "News. Mr. Sherington is bringing news. I don't know how we've only just heard but..." Frowning, she paused again.

"Well get on with it," Dulcinea said.

"There's a babe at the vicar's. Belongs to one of the village girls as followed the drum."

Dulcinea clucked her tongue. "Which one?"

The hair at the back of Fleur's neck prickled and she sent Dulcinea a quelling look. Despite relishing gossip, Mrs. Knollwood was a placid soul. Fleur had never seen her this agitated.

"That's just it," the housekeeper said. "No one knows."

"Phyllis," Fleur whispered. Helena would need to hear this possible news of her daughter and grandchild. She touched the housekeeper's arm. "Get Mrs. Bicton-Morledge dressed for callers. We'll bring them up to her sitting room."

"Oh, miss, Mr. Sherington barely made it up the few steps to the portico."

"Then we'll have James carry his mistress down."

The housekeeper wrinkled her nose. James was not quite as sturdy as the usual footmen.

"Or Captain Ardleigh can," Dulcinea said.

* * *

"You did not need to accompany me." The cross tone in Fleur's voice cheered Gareth.

He'd spent the call at Bicton Grange observing a demure Fleur chatting quietly with all and sundry and pouring tea for Mrs. Bicton-Morledge, who, with the help of Gareth's steadying arm, had waddled down the stairs for the occasion. Her daughter, Cora, a dark-haired young beauty who must be turning heads was present as well. The other two daughters, mere urchins, popped in for cakes before being shooed back to the nursery.

Lord Barlow had called on Sherington that morning with astonishing news. A child—a mere baby had been left with the vicar by an English couple who'd been visiting Toulouse. A year or so ago, the locals discovered the newborn in a barn next to the body of his mother who'd died giving birth. Miniatures of a blond-haired, blue-eyed girl and a British soldier were likely portraits of the lad's parents. The English couple brought him to Reabridge because of one more found item, an amulet. They'd recognized it as one given to Reabridge girls at the annual harvest festival.

Barlow had called out of concern that Thaddeus might have been the child's father. Neither of the Sherington men had heard Thad had married. Thaddeus wasn't likely to be the father.

As for the mother's possible identity, Mr. Sherington insisted he must personally deliver this news to Mrs. Bicton-Morledge. Gareth had been only too happy to accompany him.

Mrs. Bicton-Morledge had taken the news with quiet composure, deeming it unlikely the boy was her daughter Phyllis's. Phyllis's hair had been brown, not blond.

Still, one could see sadness and worry lurking beneath the lady's calm surface. She'd excused herself early, and Gareth had insisted on carrying her up the stairs, Cora walking alongside.

When he returned to the drawing room, Sherington was saying his farewells and Fleur was retrieving her shawl. She'd come along for the return trip to Sherington Manor with the excuse of borrowing a novel that Lady Ixworth wanted. Then, novel, in hand, she'd declined the offer of a carriage ride home.

Gareth had snatched up the book before Fleur could quick-march from Sherington Manor with it. *The Monk* was now carefully wrapped in oilcloth against the possibility of rain and tucked under his waistcoat next to his heart.

He needed this time alone with Fleur. What sort

of woman had she become? What experiences had she had? What did she want in her life? He needed to know her better before he wrote to Marceau with the news that he'd found the Frenchman's prospective bride.

At least that was his excuse.

"I confess," he said, "I was surprised to find you unmarried."

She made no reply.

Fair enough. This was Fleur, after all.

"You are accomplished and dare I say beautiful? Do the men of… Derbyshire… not have eyes in their heads?"

"Staffordshire," she said. "Eyes? Yes. Brains? Not many. But those who do know that beauty won't pay rent or buy food. At least not in the respectable way."

That was more words than he'd ever heard out of Fleur at one time, and it told him much. She had no income, and the men of Staffordshire wanted her, but not for matrimony.

"I see. Yet you and Lady Ixworth plan to return there after your visit here?"

Fleur stopped, pivoted, and studied him. "You are impertinent, Ardleigh. But then you've always been thus, haven't you?"

He supposed that was true. Yet he needed to know much more before he wrote Marceau. The Frenchman would have to know how to woo her, after all.

Good old Fleur. Ever honest—*if* he could get her to talk—and if that required frank questioning, so be it.

Perhaps he ought to apologize, but he wasn't one to grovel. "I've offended you."

"Much offends me." She grimaced. "I suppose you'll run back and share whatever I tell you with your circle of so-called gentlemen. Oh yes, I know that you men gossip as madly as any females."

Unfortunately, that was true. He thought of the many drunken conversations in the officers' mess. "Hand to heart." He touched the rectangle under his coats. A book such as this had once shielded him from a stray piece of shrapnel. "Your secrets will be my secrets."

"Hmm." That grimace again. "We have lost our home in Staffordshire. Put out by the new heir. So, no, we will not be returning there."

The last rays of the setting sun sparked diamonds in her hair and in the corners of her eyes. Incipient tears?

The notion of his Petal near tears tugged at his heart. Fleur had feelings. He'd always suspected that, but she'd always hid her hurt behind a steel cage.

By God, she was lovely, and so strong. Not at all like the Frenchwoman Marceau had been keeping. Marceau had made commitments to her that involved a two year old and another on the way, so Gareth supposed she'd been well within her rights in her weeping. What the Veuve thought of it all, Gareth didn't know.

How unfair the match with Marceau would be to Fleur.

A promise was a promise though, and his debt to the Veuve had to be repaid. He must at least introduce Fleur to Marceau.

"It's a marriage you need," Gareth said. "It will secure your future."

"Yes," she said, astonishing him. "And that of Lady Ixworth."

"Lady Ixworth?" He laughed, shocked at her agreeableness to marriage and appalled that she would attach such an unlikely requirement. "Surely she has family who—"

"She has *me*. And a small—very small—income. It's no secret that the late viscount gambled away almost everything. We will stay with Mrs. Bicton-Morledge and make ourselves useful until..." She shrugged. "She *might* have a son."

The Bicton-Morledge females' predicament was common knowledge. Those gossiping males again.

"And she might not, and then what?"

One of Fleur's long silences ensued, and she stepped out again.

He kept pace with her. "You are here husband-hunting, I take it? Don't count on Laurence. I believe he intends to sow his wild oats for a few more years.

In fact, now that his father is much improved, he's returning to London perhaps tomorrow or the day after to see to business there."

Her pace slowed. "You don't offer your own hand, Captain Ardleigh?"

CHAPTER FOUR

*F*rom any other woman, that would have been flirting, but there was a cynicism to Fleur's tone that irritated, reminding him of his own financial circumstances.

"Poor as a church mouse," he said, wishing it wasn't so.

Her lips curved in a tight smile. "You are safe with me, as is Laurence. I have no interest in finding a young husband."

"No interest… What?" He slapped a hand to his forehead. "You mean to say you're after Laurence's father?" A laugh exploded from him.

"I mean to say no such thing," she said. "But why not an older man? Someone settled, seeking companionship, less likely to gamble away everything or beat me."

"While you use your wiles to wrap him around your finger. Ah, you French women."

"I am not French. I am English. I despise all things French."

That would certainly make his task more difficult. Marceau was not a naturally charming man unless he was striking a deal with a wine merchant. It would be up to Gareth to convince Fleur to make her home in France.

"But why? There are many good people in France."

"Like the ones who killed Thaddeus?"

"That was war, Fleur. They killed us, we killed them. It's the way of things for soldiers. There's no point in holding on to resentments."

She eyed him sideways, a look of puzzlement in her gaze, and walked on.

"Don't you ever wish to visit there? You certainly have family there."

"Do I? Why have they not sought me out?" Her voice crackled with rare emotion, but the wings of her bonnet hid her face.

They have left me to do that. He could see it must be done carefully. Even the hardiest of flowers could be blown over by a strong wind.

"Perhaps… perhaps you're an heiress."

"Bah."

"What if I investigate? Look for your family? Will you promise to meet them?"

They'd reached the front steps of Bicton Grange. Fleur held out her hand. "You'll find no one. They were killed in the terror and the fighting. And those who weren't, those who supported the revolution and Bonaparte, they are dead to me. Now, please may I have the book?"

He handed it over and waited until the door opened and then closed on her.

Fleur was more resentful than most of the soldiers he knew. He turned and retraced his steps to Sherington Manor, remembering the taunts young Fleur had received from those riffraff children from Lower Reabridge. He could still feel the satisfying crack of the bigger fellow's nose under his fist.

Fleur had been hurt deeply. He ought to have realized that business of not speaking had been young Fleur's punishment against her small world. To lose her parents, to be placed with strangers, to come to a country where she was taunted about who she was… Marceau would not understand. He might well become the kind of husband who would beat her.

Walking back to Sherington Manor in the descending twilight, he passed groups of hired harvest workers heading to their rest. Some looked surlier than others, grownup versions of those bullies taunting his Petal so many years ago. It was good he'd escorted her home. At least he could offer her that sort of protection.

The rest though... The Veuve wanted this match with Marceau, and he'd promised to try to arrange it as a matter of honor.

But what of Fleur's wishes? He ought to have expected the same stubborn Fleur, grown stronger with age, but this Fleur—she was stubborn, that was true, but she was also homeless, desperate, vulnerable...

And here to find a husband. If Gareth delayed an introduction to Marceau much longer, Fleur might find someone else.

There was talk of the ladies paying a call on a family he didn't know tomorrow. Perhaps he'd look out and attach himself to their party.

* * *

"Miss Farnham is a lovely girl," Dulcinea said. "A pity Mr. Farnham was out, but I'm happy to learn that the vicar is at home today."

From her perch on the gig's cargo box, Cora chattered away about her friend, Miss Farnham, and the vicar, who was one of her guardians, and the Reabridge shops, all the while nibbling biscuits from the basket on her lap.

Fleur scarcely listened, pretending to concentrate on handling the lines. It had rained the night before, and there were muddy patches to navigate.

Besides, she was feeling low. Not only had she

been unable to meet Mr. Farnham, but she'd learned more about the orphaned child abandoned on the clueless vicar. The foolish man had sent the child's nursemaid packing, expecting various local women to care for the terrified babe. At least now he'd found a woman to live in and care for him.

But she was French.

As they approached the town, her thoughts turned to Gareth and the conversation of the previous day. She'd almost expected him to dog her steps today again, but there'd been no sign of him as they passed Sherington Manor, nor when they drove through Reabridge earlier. She must stop looking for him everywhere.

There was a reason she always chose to speak as little as possible. She'd told Gareth too much. She'd given him too many ways to taunt her.

There was also the temptation he roused in her. She'd come a hair's breadth from flirting with him. Teasing him had only led to him turning the tables and asking questions about her family in France.

Bah. France—a place where demons sporting cockades lurked behind every bush. No one in France had cared for her mother or father or bothered to look for Fleur. To Hades with them.

And the same went for Gareth Ardleigh.

The look on his face when she'd teased him about offering his own hand? She'd mustered a smile because pride had demanded it.

"The captain," Cora called over her shoulder. "He's coming up behind us. Captain Ardleigh," she shouted. "Good day to you."

"Ladies." He doffed his hat. "Where are you off to today?"

"We've just called on the Farnham's," Cora said. "Mama wanted to come, but she thought better of it and sent me along to make her apologies and to make the introductions. And now Fleur has promised to stop in the village so I may buy a new ribbon."

"Has she, Miss Cora? I declare, I shall make myself a nuisance and accompany you."

Fleur winced, refusing to look his way. She'd bet a quid he was grinning.

"But first we'll call on the vicar, Mr. Owen," Dulcinea said. "He was a regular correspondent of my late cousin. We have biscuits for him, if Miss Cora hasn't eaten all of them. If you wish, Fleur, you may set me down at the parsonage while you run off shopping."

Would it be bad of Fleur to stay at the vicarage and send Cora off shopping with the captain? Having put her daughter in the care of Fleur, Mrs. Bicton-Morledge would probably frown on the notion.

"May I join you on your mission?" Gareth asked. "I've seen Thom Owen at the Book and Bell, but I've not had a chance to call on his father."

"Oh, I hope Thom is there," Cora cried. "In any case, I must visit as well. The ribbon can wait. My mother will want a report on this baby the vicar has taken in."

As they reached the vicarage, Gareth quickly dismounted, and Cora bounced down with her basket.

"Come help me down," Dulcinea said, beckoning Gareth.

Fleur sighed and busied herself securing the lines. Dulcinea and Cora were already headed up the walk when she turned to climb down and felt Gareth's hands on her waist lifting her as if she were a child instead of a woman of two and twenty.

Her breath left her in a whoosh, heat surging from her middle, up into her cheeks, and down into...

She *must* get hold of herself. "You may release me now," she said to his black neckcloth. Raising her eyes, she saw he was frowning.

"May I? I suppose I ought to. In case anyone comes down the lane and sees us. Are you quite alright? There for a moment you seemed a bit breathless."

A corner of his mouth was turning up.

A fresh wave of heat rose in her cheeks, and she silently cursed.

"How was your quest with Mr. Farnham today?"

Mustering some composure she said, "He wasn't at home."

"What a shame." The smile tugged at the other corner of his mouth. "I suppose you'll return another day?"

Suspicion dawned. *He wouldn't have...*

Of course, he would have. This was Gareth.

"Did you have anything to do with his absence, Captain Ardleigh?"

"In point of fact, I met him last night in the taproom of the inn and we made an engagement to go riding this morning. Capital fellow and quite hardy. Still in his forties. His father lived to be eighty. Not old enough for your plans, my dear."

An angry pulse thrummed in her head. "I see. Well then." She pushed at his hands, and he quickly released her, tucking her fingers over his arm.

"You look positively blooming today, Petal," he said.

If she had her parasol in hand, she would beat him to within an inch of his life.

She mustered a breath and said, "Thank you."

The front door of the vicarage stood open. She pulled her arm from his and hurried along behind Dulcinea and Cora to the drawing room. While a manservant announced them, the people gathered there rose. The soberly dressed man must be the vicar. A woman of middling years eyed them, and a petite, dark-haired younger woman of perhaps thirty set a toddler in skirts onto the floor before standing.

Fair-haired and blue-eyed, the child looked up with the face of an angel, and then quickly dropped to his knees on the Aubusson carpet and crawled over to a scattered set of blocks.

Mr. Owen greeted Cora and introductions were made.

The French nanny, Miss Du Plessac, watched the boy as he played, looking ready to jump up and protect him. Her gown, though of good quality, was of a style more out of date than those in Fleur's wardrobe. Where on earth had the vicar found her?

"Mr. Owen," Dulcinea said, "you and I have met before when you visited my cousin Mr. Quidenham. He was kind enough to invite me to live with him after my husband died."

"Quidenham was a great correspondent of mine. We shared an interest in St. Paul's travels in Greece. I was very sorry to hear of his passing. Will you be staying in Reabridge for long?"

"We shall see," Dulcinea said. "For now, we're abiding with Mrs. Bicton-Morledge. She's just learned of the presence of young Sam. As you can imagine, we're here on her behalf."

"For what purpose?" Miss du Pessac's back stiffened and her sharp little chin came up. Cora's mouth dropped open, and the vicar opened his mouth to speak, but Fleur jumped in first.

"Her daughter, Phyllis Bicton-Morledge, followed the drum," she said, "and the family hasn't heard from her since she left three years ago. Sam may be Mrs. Bicton-Morledge's grandson. Cora might be his aunt."

The French woman's terse nod was not a friendly one.

The vicar told them about Sam's arrival in Reabridge with an English couple and repeated the story Mr. Sherington had shared with him.

"Mademoiselle," Gareth said, turning the full force of his charm on the French nursemaid, "Mr. Owen. Is it possible for Cora to see the miniatures of the couple believed to be the child's parents?"

The vicar retrieved a large locket from the mantel, opened it, and handed it to Cora.

"Oh." Cora's gaze traveled around the room ending at Fleur. "She looks more like you, Fleur, and Phyllis's husband looks nothing like this."

In that moment Sam, wide-eyed and curious appeared at Fleur's knee and presented her a block. Her heart did a flip, and the wobbly smile on the little face drew a smile out of her. "Thank you, Sam," she said.

"*De rien*," Miss du Pessac said coaxingly, reaching for the boy and drawing him up onto her lap. "He speaks some English but will understand better if you speak French."

You're not teaching him English? She closed her mouth on the words, remembering the fear and uncertainty she saw behind the child's smile. No need to stir trouble, at least not in the little boy's presence.

Gareth jumped in, conversing easily with Miss du Pessac, so easily he was almost flirting, while Fleur battled her rising irritation.

CHAPTER FIVE

*A*s Gareth escorted the ladies to their gig, Mr. Sherington passed by and hailed them from the window of his carriage. Chuckling, Gareth saluted.

It was astounding how quickly Sherington had discarded his Bath chair. Either Fleur or Lady Ixworth—and Gareth's money was on the latter— had raised George Sherington from his funk.

In fact, today Sherington insisted on taking the older lady up into his more comfortable equipage, promising to convey her back to Bicton Grange while the younger ones shopped.

"What a lucky thing that Mr. Sherington came along, and Cora met up with a friend equally enthusiastic about ribbons." They'd tied up the gig and his horse and were strolling the market square.

"I'm rather glad you and I have this time alone together," he added, squashing a smile.

He was alone with an even more silent than usual Fleur.

"Interesting morning wasn't it?" he said. "Perhaps we'll learn something more about the child very soon." The vicar had been speaking with all the families who'd lost sons in the war and had daughters unaccounted for. "I heard that he almost had a cat fight in his parlor between Mrs. Pownell and Mrs. Buckley."

"More gossiping with your gentlemen friends?"

"Yes. I suppose it was that." He smiled, but she didn't look his way.

"I at least know who my parents were," she said finally.

Ah. His heart skipped a beat. Fleur had found a bittersweet blessing in the poor lad's tale.

For his part, the mystery had induced a great deal of... Unease? Was that it? War—the relentless boredom, the sudden fierce battle, the jittery realization that one had survived—all produced unaccountable unions: soldiers with wives following the drum and suddenly widowed, soldiers with local women—taboo but inevitable, and soldiers with the usual assortment of other camp followers.

"Might Cora have been wrong?" he asked. "Might that have been her sister in the miniature?"

Fleur glanced up at him. Her eyes, gray and

luminous, looked as though storm clouds were gathering.

"I hadn't seen Phyllis since she was a child. But surely Cora is right." She chewed her lower lip. "Helena—Mrs. Bicton-Morledge—is fr-fragile."

His Petal's voice broke on that last word.

"Mrs. Bicton-Morledge? Do you care for her? She sent you away, didn't she?"

Fleur studied the window of Randall Clark's Mercantile, though he knew she wasn't looking at the crockery displayed there. "At first... well, you know what sort of child I was. I was angry, frightened. But I came to be grateful. Dulcinea —well..."

He clutched his hands behind his back, fighting the urge to hold her, waiting as she gathered her thoughts.

"Helena spoke with me about it, seeking to make amends. She fears dying in childbirth. She w-worries what will become of her girls." Her voice shook, and she turned away from him again.

He eyed her sidewise, thunderstruck. Meeting Sam had certainly stirred her, but this uncharacteristic display of emotion was not about *her* sorrows. She'd mentioned her desire to secure not just her own future but Lady Ixworth's as well. Now she'd be planning to include Mrs. Bicton-Morledge and her daughters in her marriage settlements.

He ought to have noticed before: she wore the same dress he'd seen her in yesterday, and the day before that, an unadorned lavender that might be half-mourning for Lady Ixton's cousin or for her former guardian, Bicton-Morledge. Her dress, her bonnet, the twist of her hair, were all simple and unaffected. Her half boots had scuff marks that no polish could cover. Her only jewelry was a garnet cross at her neck.

Fleur's quest for a marriage wasn't solely about money to save herself. She would sacrifice herself on the altar of a loveless marriage to save Lady Ixton and all of the Bicton-Morledge girls as well should the very worst happen.

Touch his heart it might—and it did—but it also spelled trouble for his matchmaking endeavor. Marceau wouldn't take in a whole passel of females of all ages, nor would the Veuve support it. The lady had barely come to tolerate him, a British officer. He didn't fool himself that it was his charming personality; the Veuve had a mercenary streak, and he was useful to her.

"When is the babe due?"

"It ought to arrive in October. But she is grown so very big... These things are not always easy to determine."

The child's birth would be a day of reckoning for the household of women.

"Surely the heir won't put her and her girls out," he said. At least not immediately.

She shrugged. "Perhaps not, but from what she tells me about him, he certainly won't allow Dulcinea and me to stay."

He hadn't written to Marceau yet. There was time. The Frenchman's last letter had mentioned negotiations with wine merchants and the possibility of traveling to Manchester for an auction. His London host had steered him toward the best evening entertainment, and he was availing himself of the most discerning establishments for gentlemen.

In other words, Marceau was visiting every decent brothel in London, steeling himself for the upcoming nuptials. Having thought to eventually gain the Veuve's approval of a marriage to his amour, he'd bristled at the notion of an arranged marriage to a cousin no one knew. His mistress's tiresome weeping and the Veuve's nagging had brought about his final agreement.

Fleur was only a year or two younger than Marceau, but she was much older in other ways. The Frenchman didn't have the disposition for a strong wife, much less a strong wife with Lady Ixworth in tow.

A sickening feeling swept over him. Honor was important, and he'd defended his own ardently all through his young years, mostly with his fists, only once with a sword. But this... this marriage? Debt of honor or no, Marceau shouldn't have Fleur. It wouldn't do. He'd travel to France himself and explain all to the Veuve.

And Fleur... she could travel with him and meet her grandmother. Lady Ixworth could come as well. Neither lady would expect luxury; he could sell one of his precious bottles to pay their passage.

"That poor lad," Fleur said, interrupting his planning, "Perhaps his father is still alive." She stopped and frowned up at him. "*Could* he be Thad's?"

"Unless Thad was secretly married, no."

"You would know if he'd married, wouldn't you?"

"I... I lost touch with him quite often. We served in different regiments and for a time... well, I was captured by the French."

Her gaze skittered over him. "*Captured?*" She stopped dead and put her hands to her hips. "Captured, Gareth?"

"Yes."

"Did they... harm you?"

He drew in a breath, a memory flashing, quickly squashed. He'd never been one for grudges or crying the victim. In fact, he'd had it easier than many others. "No, no not really. Oh, there was a bit of thrashing about, but their commander soon saw that I was an officer and a gentleman."

"And tried to wheedle secrets out of you."

Yes, he'd first been beaten and then charmed. "It didn't work, if you're wondering."

She eyed him up and down. "I never thought to ask—besides the scar on your jaw, were you wounded?"

Wounded? More likely than not, he'd carry the shrapnel of battle to his death along with various scars. But most of those, of course, he'd received earlier, in Spain. A French surgeon had kindly and cleanly removed the only bullet he'd received. "Only a few scratches."

"You were beaten and tortured, and yet not injured?"

He shrugged. "As it happened, I escaped."

Was this the right time to bring up Etienne Marceau?

"I was helped by a Frenchman and his old aunt. They took me in, hid me, tended my, er, scratches."

Her mouth dropped open and then she frowned. "You *were* wounded, Gareth. How long were you with *those people*?"

"A mere few weeks. And the wounds were nothing. I was lucky. Very lucky. The French are not all bad, you see."

"Huh," she said with disgust.

"No." He caught her arm, stopping her, and drawing her into an opening between two buildings. "I like the French generally. And in particular," he touched his fingers to her jaw, "I like you."

A tiny gasp escaped her. "I am not—"

"But you are. And certainly, you have family there."

"No." She pushed past him and hurried back to the square.

"Thank you for reminding me why I must marry," she said, bristling with anger as he caught up with her. "I am French by birth, but as soon as I marry an Englishman, I will take my husband's citizenship."

"So who is it to be? Sherington? Farnham?"

"Perhaps whoever takes the baby will need a nursemaid… But no. That Miss du Plessac will have the position."

"Perhaps. But… I've heard rumors that she and the vicar's son are engaged."

She stopped and her brows drew together. "If that's so, I might yet find work."

"Have you ever cared for a small child?"

"Only Phyllis and Cora when all of us were little."

"And if you're a nursemaid, what of Lady Ixworth?"

"Sherington likes Dulcinea. We might both have a home." She threw up her hands. "I'm grasping at straws I suppose."

"Well there is still Mr. Farnham," he teased. "Perhaps he'll be smitten and offer for you."

He thought it unlikely. Farnham had spoken

fondly of his late wife. He didn't seem like a man in search of a new one.

"Is Mr. Farnham sensible?"

"I suppose so. Obsessed with his drainage. We rode all about his acres. Fascinating stuff, if you like that sort of thing." His own family estate was on higher ground. Most vineyards were as well.

"Financially stable?"

"I didn't poke into finances."

"Handsome?"

Mr. Farnham was, in fact a lean hardy man who appeared to have all his hair and teeth.

"I'm no judge of that, I'm afraid."

Fleur snorted and waved. Cora and her friend had stepped out of a shop.

"I'll bid you farewell, Captain."

A tall man dressed in laborer's clothing stopped Cora and tipped his hat. There was something familiar about him.

Cora smiled up at the fellow. Even from here, Gareth could see she was flirting.

"Who is that?" Gareth asked. "He's awfully friendly with Miss Cora."

Fleur shaded her eyes and an assessing look came over her. "You don't recognize him? That's Bevan Haskell. He manages the crews of itinerant harvest workers. He's visited the steward at Bicton Grange to arrange the wages, and even paid a call on Helena."

"Cora oughtn't to be so familiar with him. And you—after the way he treated you?"

"We were children then. And... as for Cora, well, Haskell has a reputation as a hard worker. After his father died, he held the family together. He has a freehold he shares with a brother-in-law, and he's respected in the community."

"He's a brute and beneath her station." He stepped out to cross the square, but Fleur's hand stayed him.

"Don't," she said. "Helena is not any more concerned about him than any other young man. He's not likely to whisk her off to follow the drum."

Haskell had spotted them. He lifted his hat, said a few words to Cora, and departed.

"There now," she said, "he's gone, and I see Cora has a package. She and I will be off. Haskell is a man with important work to do, and Cora and I have duties to attend to. You may go as well and be about whatever your business is."

He winced at her dig. It was true, he was taking a break from soldiering, but he had important business of another sort.

She wouldn't get rid of him that quickly. "I'll ride along beside you and gather the latest gossip from Cora to share with Sherington, and perhaps stop at the Book and Bell later for more news. Someone might know something about the lad's parents."

"Intelligence gathering. Did you do a bit of that during the war?"

In fact, he'd been on a mission when he was captured. A long moment passed, and she scoffed. "Silence, Captain Ardleigh? Well then, I'll be careful to guard the names of the gentlemen I'll be calling on, so you don't get to them first *again*. Unless you'd be willing to help me? Surely somewhere in England there's a man for me."

"And for your elderly companion."

"In fact, Dulcinea has just turned two and sixty, and she is healthier than many ladies half her age, and still very attractive. She's kept her figure as well."

Lady Ixworth did look well for her age, but the only lady whose figure interested him was the one next to him. He took her hand and set it over his arm, itching to touch more, to wrap his arm around her waist and feel again the softness where her hip curved.

Alas, there was another man for Fleur, Etienne Marceau, if she'd have him. With him, she'd have the security of family, and an entrée into a prosperous business. She'd have a husband who wasn't likely to leave her, but who would cheat like the devil on her and never love her.

If Gareth would allow Etienne Marceau to have her. Because, God's truth, he wanted her for himself. Fleur ought to be his. She ought to be not just taken to wife, she ought to be loved.

* * *

WHILE HE RODE SILENTLY AND FLEUR DEFTLY handled the gig, Cora told them about the plans for the Harvest festival the following weekend. On Saturday, the booths would go up on the green. On Sunday, there'd be a special afternoon church service, and following that, some of the landowners would hold dinners. On Monday, there'd be a parade of wagons, a fair, and dancing. There'd be Morris dancers, games, booths, and a grand bonfire.

For the second time this day, Gareth became lost in his thoughts, something he generally avoided at all costs. The cropped fields and hedgerows they passed brought to mind other hedges he'd dragged his injured self in and out of, hiding from the French.

When the hedgerows of Champagne ended, the road ran along sweeps of trellised vines, the naked twists sporting green buds here or there. At the sound of an approaching cart, he'd staggered into a row where he must have fainted. The next thing he knew, a strong, wiry Frenchman was half dragging him along, all the while cursing under his breath about a woman.

Struggling for one last gasp of strength to break free, Gareth spotted a cart. It wasn't a gendarme holding the lines, not unless they were enlisting old women.

She railed at the young man to put the stranger into the cart bed, and then to cover him with a scratchy tarp in case of patrols. Once horizontal, Gareth succumbed to the blackness again and woke up in a creaky cot on a lumpy mattress in a room warmed by a small brazier. It felt enough like heaven that he'd slept for three days straight.

He discovered his wounds had been tended to, his clothing cleaned, and a covered dish and flask of wine left on the side table for him.

Etienne Marceau had saved him from the peril of a cold hungry night passed out in the vineyard. Not so much because he'd wanted to; Marceau's great aunt, the Veuve Hardouin had demanded it.

At this point of the war, helping an enemy officer held little risk for them. Marceau had been too young for the Jacobin madness. Later, he'd avoided conscription in the Grande Armée by keeping his emperor supplied with champagne from the family winery. The Veuve was no fool; she could see the end of the war coming. She'd staged cargo in the lowlands, awaiting an armistice, and seized the opportunity to forge bonds with an English officer who could help Hardouin and Marceau weather the precarious time between armistice and a return to peace and the expansion of their trade.

Plus, Gareth's death in the vineyard might have spoiled the next year's harvest.

He chuckled to himself.

"What's funny?" Cora called, shaking him out of his reverie. "Oh look. They've finished the north field."

The brisk autumn air carried the scent of freshly mowed barley, bringing old memories of his family home, and more recent ones of Champagne where he'd immersed himself as fully as possible for a sheltering enemy soldier in the operations of the vineyard.

He'd risen from his sickbed and joined the Veuve and her nephew for meals, conscious of the need to attempt to contact his regiment. Before he could do so, news came, first of the emperor's defeat at Toulouse, and then of his surrender. Meals and conversations had led to tours and chats with the Veuve's workers, and a few months later, a visit during the height of the harvest. He'd pitched in and helped, relishing the excitement of harvest, the soreness and sense of accomplishment after a day of physical labor.

At some point, he'd remembered a little girl with the surname of Hardouin, setting in motion his current quandary.

He was in love with Fleur.

He was in love with Fleur. He, with his two hundred pounds a year. His family didn't have room for him, much less a wife and children if he married.

He thought of the softness of Fleur under her garments. There would be children, plural.

He wanted to marry her. It was madness. There'd be no champagne for them. They'd be scrimping to have a roof over their heads and food on the table. It would be foolish, reckless, irresponsible.

"Captain, you've passed the turn off for Sherington Manor," Cora called, breaking him out of this particular reverie.

"Why so I have," he said. "I believe I'll just ride along the rest of the way and call on your mother."

"You don't have to," Cora said, subdued. "She'll be resting today. Yesterday about did her in. She was worried but... I don't think the girl in that locket was Phyllis. Nor did the soldier look like her William. William had dark hair like yours, Captain."

"You met him?"

"Oh yes. The militia camped near here and came to all the village fêtes. He was very kind. When he offered for Phyllis, Papa said they must wait."

"But they didn't."

"They married in Scotland. That's all we know."

Another foolish jump into matrimony.

It wasn't a leap he would take. In the long run, it wouldn't be kind. It wouldn't be honorable. He'd write the letter summoning Marceau to Reabridge as soon as he returned to Sherington Manor.

CHAPTER SIX

With the Bicton Grange housekeeper, Mrs. Knollwood, beside her, Fleur set out early the next day in the gig, leaving Cora and Dulcinea behind to keep company with Helena and see to household matters.

They would first do some shopping, and then address the more important business. Mrs. Knollwood had known all the Bicton-Morledge girls since they were wee things and having grown up in Reabridge she'd known many of the girls who'd left the village. She'd asked Helena for leave to see the baby everyone was talking about and view the locket. They would pay a call at the vicarage.

"It's glad I am, miss, that you and your lady have come to stay with us," Mrs. Knollwood said. "It does a heart good to see my mistress is not alone. Mayhap it's not my place, but her own family could have done more. Will have to if this child is not a boy."

"I recall her mother visiting her," Fleur said. Helena's mother had showered Phyllis and her baby brother and sister with affection and completely ignored *the French girl*.

"Passed away some years ago, her mother did. My mistress's brother was killed in France, and her only sister is in India."

Fleur had forgotten about the brother killed in the early days of the war. No wonder Helena's mother had shunned her.

"'Struth and I hope that this child is not Phyllis's," Mrs. Knollwood said, "for 'twould mean Phyllis is lost to us entirely."

"A sad thought that. Cora feels certain the babe is not Phyllis's. When was the last time anyone heard from her?"

"'Twas a few months after she left. She'd married in Scotland, and then she and her man had sailed for Spain to rejoin his regiment."

"That they married was some comfort, I suppose."

"Oh, aye. Her mother's heart wasn't broken entirely. Her da ought to have let them marry, I say. It's all well and good to be practical, but young William was a good lad." She drew in a breath. "What of you, Miss Hardouin? Are you hoping to marry?"

She turned over several answers in her mind. She

could set the housekeeper in her place, but that seemed inordinately missish.

Mrs. Knollwood wasn't a malicious gossip, nor had she ever been unkind.

"Yes," Fleur said. "I fear I must."

"If I do say so, miss, Captain Ardleigh seems very attentive."

Gareth. Despite the chill autumn air, warmth surged in her. "Captain Ardleigh?" she said, managing a bland tone.

Mrs. Knollwood shifted on the seat. "Such a jolly young man."

Fleur pretended that a difficult patch of road required all her attention.

"So handsome too," the housekeeper said. "I recall him as a goodhearted lad."

They had reached the bridge to the island. "Yes," Fleur said, "he was kind to me as a child. Now, let us see if the vicar is home."

* * *

GARETH PACED THE FOUR WALLS OF THE BICTON Grange parlor, listening to the distant wails and screeches from the nursery floor.

The distracted maid answering the door had ushered him here and hurried out, promising to fetch someone without ever asking Gareth who he was calling on.

When the door creaked, Lady Ixworth entered, back straight, head regal, and a smile on her face that he'd call cheeky—perhaps even devious.

She was a lively one for an older lady. He understood why Sherington admired her so.

He crossed the room and greeted her.

"She's gone into the village." Lady Ixworth curved her hand around his arm and brushed her shoulder against his. "She took the housekeeper along in the gig. Helena is resting, the little girls are in the schoolroom arguing, Cora is in the kitchen, and so, you have me to keep you company."

They'd reached a sofa, and she seated herself, patting the cushion next to her. "Do sit. Or do you want to run after Fleur?"

Her face had grown solemn, reminding him of his warmhearted granny when she had to administer discipline. He couldn't help grinning. "Why do I sense a scold coming?"

"I never scold, Captain Ardleigh. I state what I think dispassionately."

"Ah." She was much like Fleur. "Well, then, perhaps I'm in for an interrogation?"

She raised her eyebrows and looked down her nose at him, rather like Wellington the one time he'd been in his lordship's lofty presence.

"You have my full attention, my lady."

"Fleur means to marry."

"So she has told me."

"And you, Captain? Do you mean to marry?"

"Do I mean to marry?" Irritation had crept into his voice. He cleared his throat. He was usually better at concealing his feelings. "I fear my income—"

"Is small." She waved a hand. "But you have a profession. And if there are no wars for you to fight, you are healthy and have a good head on your shoulders. You can find a position. Sherington speaks highly of you." She pursed her lips. "My gel isn't entirely penniless, you know. She has a pittance of an income her guardian preserved for her."

Fleur had more than that. She had a family in France well on their way to wealth, a family that wanted to reclaim her. He stood and paced to the fireplace.

He'd planned to write to Marceau the previous evening, but when he returned to Sherington Manor, a letter from Marceau had awaited him. Fleur's cousin would arrive in Reabridge in time for the harvest festival.

He needed to speak with Fleur before then, and before he shared her secrets with anyone else, even this lady who cared so much for her.

A rap on his arm brought his gaze back to Lady Ixworth. "Since you're being intentionally obtuse today, let me be direct: you're showing my gel a great deal of attention. Do you intend to offer for her?"

A bead of perspiration crept under his neckcloth. He returned to his seat on the sofa.

"Fleur has prospects beyond an impoverished soldier. I've just come from France and... I must speak to her first about the matter."

"Prospects? In France?" She shook her head. "I doubt her practical notions about marriage will cross the English Channel. Especially not when her heart is engaged here."

"With whom?"

The lady raised an eyebrow.

With himself? Could that possibly be true?

"If you mean me, you're mistaken. She's never expressed any, er, interest. In fact, she's often sniping at me."

"Would Fleur wear her heart on her sleeve?"

"Where you are concerned, ma'am, she certainly does."

"Hah." She shook her head. "It's because I love her as she is. I know not to expect sweetness and light in my gel's words. But her actions? Ah. Look to her actions, sir."

"She's proclaimed an intention to marry an older, well-established man. And I am neither of those. She doesn't want me. In fact, she's avoiding me."

Lady Ixworth shook her head. "You are acting the dolt. Of course, she's avoiding you. She finds you too tempting, and she's taking the easy way out." She stood and made a shooing motion. "Now get you gone. Find her and tell her about these prospects in France. And then be prepared to duck when she boxes your ears."

"She hates France that much?"

"So she says. Claims she doesn't remember the language, though her mother certainly must have spoken it to her, and she's refused to be fashionable and learn it."

The Veuve Hardouin was another strong-willed lady. He'd recalled her pleasure at his own fluent French. For her granddaughter not to speak it? She'd tolerate the insult to her country, but she'd hate the snub to the mother tongue.

As it happened, he didn't have far to go to find Fleur, but encountered her and the housekeeper in their gig returning to the Grange.

Mr. Farnham rode alongside, escorting them.

"Captain Ardleigh, well met," he called.

Gareth reined up and lifted his hat.

Fleur murmured a greeting, her expression blank. The older lady seated next to her, Bicton Grange's housekeeper, dipped her head and looked equally stoic.

"I'm off to pay a call at Sherington," Farnham said. "Are you headed that way?"

. . .

FLEUR WATCHED THE EMOTIONS PLAY ACROSS Gareth's handsome face. He looked positively ashen this morning, as if he'd received bad news, and his normal sure-footed jolliness had been replaced with uncertainty and hesitation.

He wanted time with her and that was the one thing she couldn't stomach right now.

Mr. Farnham was *interested* in her. She could feel it down to her baby toes. And he was—or might be—perfect for her. He was ruggedly handsome in an older sort of way, well-spoken and seemingly intelligent, and had legs that would meet with Dulcinea's approval.

She must avoid time alone with Gareth. Must, must, must. If he touched her as he'd done yesterday… if he kissed her, if he asked for her hand…

Of course, he wouldn't. He couldn't. Her plan was a good one. She must follow through with it.

"Do run along, Captain Ardleigh," she said. "I have promised to spend the afternoon with the girls in the schoolroom."

"Working on their French?" he asked.

Her knuckles whitened around the lines she was gripping. "Needlework," she said.

His face relaxed into the start of a grin and his eyes brightened. "Ah. Embroidery. I recall that was a specialty of yours."

That dreadful handkerchief. How had he remembered?

Oh, but it touched her heart that he did, and embarrassed her too. Though she'd been awfully proud of it, it had been a clumsy piece of work. "More likely we will be darning ripped frocks and torn stockings." She clucked and the horses moved on.

So what that he remembered her farewell gift? He'd no doubt chucked it into the nearest privy as soon as he'd waved goodbye.

She glanced behind her and saw his proud back moving down the lane.

The wind blew a chill under her shawl, and she bit her lip, straightened her shoulders and drove on.

AT BICTON GRANGE, FLEUR HURRIED TO GRAB HER workbasket, and found Dulcinea exiting Helena's bedchamber.

"She's resting," Dulcinea said. "I declare, seeing Helena's discomfort, I'm glad Ixworth never got me with child. Bring your work and come along to the parlor. Cook has all the girls in the kitchen baking cakes for the festival."

Dulcinea made her way to a fireside chair in the parlor and settled in. "Now, have a look at this note."

Fleur unfolded the paper, scanned the first line, and looked up. "It's an invitation to dinner tonight at

Sherington Hall. From Sherington, not Mrs. Smythe, and addressed *My Dear Dulcy*. Is there something you haven't told me?" She held the paper to her nose and sniffed it.

Dulcinea turned her gaze to the fire, a wicked smile forming.

Fleur glanced at the rest of the note. Laurence had returned to London, but Captain Ardleigh and Mr. Farnham would join them.

"I see. Did you reply?"

"We are going. Did you meet Mr. Farnham today?"

"Yes."

"And?"

Fleur shrugged. "On the face of things, he is highly unobjectionable."

Dulcinea laughed merrily. "My gel," she said, wiping tears. "Oh my gel. In any case, you must wear the primrose gown."

"But that is your—"

"It's yours now. It will show the man you have a bosom worth looking at."

Fleur sighed and poked through her basket. "Then I must fix the hole in my best stockings."

* * *

FARNHAM LEFT GARETH AT THE SHERINGTON MANOR stables, saying he would be up at the house a bit later to call on Sherington. After seeing to his mount, Gareth stopped in the kitchens, wheedled a sandwich and small beer from Cook, and was dusting off crumbs when the butler found him and summoned him to the study where Mr. Sherington was waiting.

It was just as well. He needed to tell him about the upcoming appearance of a Frenchman in Reabridge. Not that he'd expect Sherington to host Marceau. He'd never ask that of them.

When he pushed open the door, he saw that George Sherington had visitors. His elderly steward, Mr. Chigwell, sat across from him, while a weather-worn man in boots and well-worn coats stood. Haskell was here.

"You needed me, sir?" Gareth asked.

"Ardleigh. There you are," Sherington said.

Chigwell rose and exchanged greetings. Haskell's gaze was assessing.

"Meet Haskell," Sherington said cheerfully.

Well, of course, he didn't know of that fistfight so many years earlier.

"He's in charge of the hired workers," Sherington added.

Gareth's shoulders tensed, but he extended a hand. "We've met before." Haskell's grip was firm but not threatening.

"Aye," Haskell said. "Ye gave me this some years back." He rubbed the crook in the bridge of his nose.

"And well you deserved it," Gareth said in a pleasant tone.

The fellow's lips quirked; in the start of a smile or a grimace, Gareth couldn't discern.

Let the ass try himself on Fleur again; he'd crack more than his beak.

"Your men have done well," Sherington said. "Haskell, let Chigwell know when they've finished that last field."

"Aye, sir, and then I'll get you a final accounting," Chigwell said. "Now, begging your pardon, I promised I'd show Mr. Farnham that drainage work needing done. He has some thoughts on it."

Chigwell and Haskell departed and Sherington directed Gareth to a chair.

"Laurence has gone up to town," Sherington said without preamble.

"Town?" Memories of the fight with the Haskells had driven out all other thoughts. The satisfying crunch of the bully's nose; Thad jumping in to fight Haskell's brother; Laurence shrinking back like the bullies' sister.

Damn, but he missed Thaddeus Sherington.

He cleared his throat. "Do you mean London, sir?"

"He's keeping close watch on the 'Change. War's over—for good this time, we hope, and things will be volatile. He's not much for the land, and there it is. If Thaddeus had lived..."

Mr. Sherington tapped the desktop. "What are your plans, lad?"

"Sir?"

"Back to your family in Derbyshire? Or back to the army? Or somewhere else?"

Somewhere else, if you please. He thought of the rolling hectares of brimming vines; the chalk caverns filled with racks of riddling bottles; late evening meals under warm skies.

That would be Fleur's life—if she'd take it. Impossible for himself.

"I'll pay my brother a short visit, of course." The shorter the better. "The army will take me back on full pay, I'm sure." If he wished to risk yellow fever or typhus in some far-flung station.

A long moment passed, and he realized Sherington was watching him.

The older man smiled. "In short, you've not decided."

Gareth laughed. "That's the long and the short of it."

"Chigwell wants to retire. While you're considering the army or the somewhere else, think about staying at Sherington Manor and working for me, as my steward. I'm offering it to you first."

He sat straighter. Sherington was a much larger property with a much larger income than the Ardleigh family estate. The land was good, the tenants stable, the park filled with small game, and the stream that cut through brimming with fish.

"When I say staying at Sherington Manor, I mean living in the manor house until Chigwell vacates his cottage, which he plans to do soon and move closer to one of his children. It's a good-sized dwelling. You can find a wife and fill your nursery."

A blush needled its way up from under his neckcloth. He cleared his throat again. "Very generous, sir." And very managing. Sherington had a matchmaker's glint in his eyes. It was the sort of thing Gareth had encountered from regimental wives with marriageable daughters, but from his old friend's father?

Gareth swallowed a chuckle. "And who did you have in mind, sir?" Not cousin, Esther, please.

Sherington raised an eyebrow. "Are you being coy with me, lad?"

"Never, sir."

Sherington laughed. "You were always a rascal. Well, then. Fetch a bottle of that *Hardouin* champagne and your saber. I'll see this sabrage Laurence was crowing about, and we'll have a chat."

CHAPTER SEVEN

*J*ealousy gnawed at Gareth as he watched Fleur at dinner.

She'd donned a yellow gown that skimmed just over the top of where her nipples must be in a delectable revelation of breasts he'd only speculated about.

She'd done something with her hair as well, with curls and braids twining here and there among pearly beads.

And it was all for Farnham, who to his credit was trying to avoid staring at Fleur's bosom.

Damnation.

While opening the champagne that afternoon, Gareth seized the opportunity to tell Sherington how he'd obtained so many cases. It was a story he'd only hinted at before, deflecting Laurence's questions.

Today he'd told him the tale: his capture, his escape, his rescue by the Veuve, the upcoming visit by Etienne Marceau, and Fleur's kinship with the family.

He hadn't quite told him the full truth of the arrangements for marriage, but Sherington must have intuited it. When Gareth spoke of his plans to ride over to Bicton Grange that afternoon and speak with Fleur, Sherington said he had a better idea. Fleur was coming to dinner, and they'd be allowed a private conversation. He added that he could see Gareth cared for her, but before he could say more, Farnham appeared.

Some plan this was that Sherington had concocted, with Fleur attired like a society lady and batting her eyelashes at Farnham.

He glanced up the table and saw Sherington's sly grin. Gareth picked up his fork, addressed the fine piece of trout on his plate, and took up his conversational duty with his dinner partner, Cousin Esther.

"Whist," Sherington proclaimed. "Shall we play ladies against gentlemen? Farnham, you're with me. Dulcy and Esther will oppose us. We shall have our work cut out for us, Farnham, for I know both ladies to be wicked good card sharps."

Sherington didn't look his way, but he knew this

was his chance. He took Fleur's hand and tucked it over his arm. "Shall we take a turn about the gallery?"

"Why not fetch us a bottle of champagne, lad?" Sherington said. "Gareth has not returned from France empty handed, Farnham. Go along, Miss Hardouin, and see my cellars. The captain is on good terms with my butler. He'll serve as chaperon."

Gareth snatched up a candle and hurried her out, ignoring her sputtering objection. When the door of the drawing room closed, he paused in the chilly hall.

The twilight filtering in through the floor length windows illuminated her breasts, the twin globes rising and falling, sending his heart racing.

He looked around. No servants lingering—they were alone.

They could go to the cellar with Sherington's ancient butler tottering behind them.

Or they could go to the place where his most exceptional wine was stored. There they'd have privacy.

And temptation. *Yes.* Just one taste of her lips before he lost her. That's what he wanted.

Fleur's gaze fixed on him, her eyes luminous, her full lips trembling.

Fleur trembling? His protective instincts stirred.

She was saving herself for marriage; he could respect that. And blast it all, she would be safe with him, though it might kill him. He'd claim one kiss, if she'd let him, but he'd never hurt her.

He took her hand and led her up the grand staircase and down a long corridor to his bedchamber.

* * *

FLEUR'S HAND AND ARM AND SHOULDER TINGLED where the parts of her touched the parts of him, and her breath came in short bursts. Her free hand itched to pull her bodice higher, though she'd tried that in private without success. All through dinner, she'd caught him watching her. Each time his eyes slid down her face and neck to her décolletage, heat spurted down to her nether regions. She was heady and jittery and, now that they were away from the safety of their older companions, filled with anticipation.

An answering tension radiated from him. Wherever they were going, he was going to try to kiss her, and maybe more.

She'd been kissed before by some of Quidenham's more devious guests. She'd even deflected attempts at the *maybe more* from the so-called gentlemen. On occasion, she'd experienced *tingles.*

But never like this. She'd never experienced

this…this…magnetic pull, this urge to throw off all caution—along with this indecent gown.

He opened a door and nudged her inside, still holding her hand.

A bedchamber. Too breathless to speak, she squinted until her eyes adjusted to the room's dimness. A discarded waistcoat draped a chair, and a man's brush and toiletries rested atop a side table. Embers smoldered in the fireplace, ready to be stirred. This was *his* bedchamber.

Her heart beat a frenzied tattoo. "Gareth," she said on the first breath she managed. He was going to make love to her.

Behind her the door snicked closed, and his hot breath touched her neck.

Perhaps *she* would make love to *him*.

She must not. What of Mr. Farnham, playing cards below?

Oh, Hades, Mr. Farnham had barely looked at her bosom, and that one glance had been not a bit spine-tingling. He'd made no declaration of interest tonight, much less courtship.

Gareth's familiar scent—shaving soap and brandy and tobacco—floated around her. She closed her eyes and savored it.

A kiss. A kiss wouldn't ruin her.

"Gareth." She swallowed and hugged herself. He moved away, set aside the candle, and returned.

"I'm not… Oh Fleur." He nudged her arms open and took her hands.

A speechless Gareth was a sight to see. His dark gaze sent her insides melting, sensation curling through her. She freed a hand and traced the scar etching his square jaw, watching his eyes darken and glitter. His was a strong face, usually a jolly one, probably a hard one when he was fighting, but not with her. The boy he was, the man he'd become, were not so very different.

"Dear Gareth," she said. Her shawl slipped from her shoulders, and she let it.

His mouth softened and he touched his thumb to her lips. "Dear Fleur."

Her hand slid from his jaw to the back of his neck. Her heels lifted her closer. Her lips sought his and pressed against them, softly, secured in a tender embrace.

His hand skimmed her waist and settled upon her back, the other wandering lower and pulling her against him. He angled his head, deepened the kiss, and breached the barrier of her lips.

Mon dieu. A shaky moment passed wherein she tasted brandy so potent it burned through her like liquid heat. She surrendered and then gave back with all of her heart.

When his lips left hers, she muttered a protest until she felt the soft press on her neck, and groaned. The hand on her bum pulled her even tighter, the other slid under her breast, and then up, stroking her through her gown until her nipples became hard points, every gentle caress echoing in her nether parts. She was burning, burning.

The bed—let's go to the bed.

Gareth's mouth stilled against her breast. A growl escaped his lips. He straightened and brushed her cheek. "We mustn't, Fleur."

She'd spoken the words aloud.

Fleur held her breath while he tucked her breast away and straightened her bodice with his long deft fingers. Gareth was right, of course, but why should he be right? Why shouldn't they... why shouldn't she...

She swallowed. Of course, she had others to think of, not just her own desires.

He picked up her shawl and draped it over her. "How beautiful you are tonight, Petal. I confess, I couldn't help myself."

Petal—the cheeky pet name brought her further back to reality.

"Come." She heard the shakiness in his voice. He cleared his throat. "I have something I must show you."

"In your bedchamber, Gareth?"

"Actually," he said tugging her along to a door near the fireplace, "in my dressing room." At the door, he stopped and pulled her shawl higher around her shoulders, casting a dazed glance at her breasts. "There's no heat in there."

A closed trunk and a chest of drawers sat against one wall, wooden crates against another, and against a third, a cot with a thin mattress and a folded blanket.

"Your valet is very tidy."

"I have no valet."

He set the candles upon a wooden crate and lifted the lid on the one next to it. Fleur pushed up next to him to look. Rows of bottles lined up neatly in a grouping of twelve.

"The champagne," she said.

"Not just any champagne, Fleur." He lifted a bottle and dusted the neck with those long bare fingers, sending another frisson of longing through her.

She shook herself.

"This is the *vin de comête* of 1811."

Wine of the comet.

"This wine, it's fantastic." He blew a kiss to the case. "It's said that the comet affected the grapes that year."

"I know of the comet." In fact, she'd seen the great comet of 1811 herself when it was visible over England around harvest time. Dulcinea's dilettante cousin had been in his astronomy phase, all abuzz about the event. He'd allowed her a look through his telescope.

"But there's more to tell you." He moved the

candles closer and lifted the paper label tied by a string to the bottle.

His hands trembled. Her gaze met his, and she caught a troubled look.

"The label. Look closely."

Squiggly, ornate cursive circled around a central name in large, bold letters: *Veuve Hardouin.*

Below that in small letters the label proclaimed *Hardouin and Marceau.*

"And so?" They were no relation to her. She had no relatives.

Gareth cradled the bottle so tenderly, irritation stabbed at her. "The Veuve—the Widow Hardouin, Fleur, she's your grandmother. It's true. It was she who rescued me when I was all but done for. When I told her I'd once met a little girl named Fleur Hardouin, she showed me a miniature of your mother, and I thought... As a little girl you resembled her. And now, you look just like her. The Veuve asked me to find you. She wants to meet you."

Stunned speechless, Fleur stared at his simply tied neck cloth, unadorned with the sort of bejeweled stickpins other men affected. He'd remembered her surname, after so many years. She blinked back a surge of moisture.

He gentled the bottle into its case and took her hand. "I thought it would be difficult to find you but... She wants to meet you."

"The Veuve Hardouin."

"Yes."

"Who believes she's my grandmother." It certainly couldn't be true. "She's mistaken, I'm sure."

"The Veuve is one of the most famous winemakers in France. Inventor of remuage—er, riddling we call it in English. Ridding the wine of sediment. It's fascinating, and it was her idea. The bottles, you see, are stored at an angle and then turned a fraction every day. Simple, but effective. Did your father or mother never speak of her?"

She shook off his hand and tugged her shawl closer, wishing she could throw it over her head and disappear. It was cold in this dressing room, and dark in the dim candlelight. No wonder he stored his precious wine here—it was almost as cold and dark as the cellars.

A flash of memory left her breathless. The scents of jasmine and grapes, a woman's soft shoulder, cold darkness. She slowed her breathing and straightened her back.

"No," she said. She knew almost nothing of her father. Angered that he'd dumped them in Bern, her mother had never spoken of him. Bicton-Morledge's report said he'd died at Lyon under the guillotine.

"Fleur, there was a man with the Veuve when she rescued me, Etienne Marceau, her great nephew. Though the business still carries his family name as well, the Marceaus have only a small stake left."

Who cared about this Etienne Marceau? He'd be

only a distant relation, if he were any relation at all. The Veuve Hardouin would be her father's mother. If *she* were any relation at all.

She wants to meet you.

Her insides were trembling. She shook her head. "I'm not traveling to France."

"Fleur." He pressed a finger to her chin and lifted it, a determined look in his eye. He'd put the precious bottle aside and was preparing to turn the full force of his charm upon her.

Moisture pooled in her eyes, unbidden and unwelcome.

"You don't have to, at least, not right away. Your cousin, Etienne Marceau, is in England. He brought cargo and has been in London dealing with wine merchants and auctions. He's coming to Reabridge for the harvest festival. And most especially, to meet you."

At those last words, Gareth had winced.

And then she knew. Gareth hadn't been interfering with her marriage plans because he wanted her for himself. He was attempting to match her with this Frenchman.

Rage pounded through her. She drew herself up, hands clenched against more trembling, jaw aching. "I shall meet him," she said, "to settle this madness. Does he speak English?"

"Some."

"Dulcinea shall translate for me. And I shall write

a letter for him to carry to this widow and ask her..." she took in a breath.

Why didn't you come for me?

She shook off the self-pity. Would this Veuve share with her the bounties of war? If the house was famous enough, there must be those.

Imagine—she and Dulcinea, English women supported by the profits of Napoleon's wine-swilling?

"I'd much rather grovel to a stuffy English husband than to an old Frenchwoman."

She turned and fled the room with as much dignity as she could muster.

* * *

THE NEXT DAY, AND THE DAYS FOLLOWING, FLEUR HAD no choice but to keep herself busy. While Dulcinea sat with Helena, all able hands were needed in the kitchen, still room, and herb garden, even those of the little Bicton-Morledge girls. Haskell stopped in more than once, passing through the kitchen on his way to the steward's office, making a point to exchange pleasantries with Cora. Cora's blushes told Fleur his interest was welcomed.

She still wasn't sure she approved. The Bicton-Morledges were solidly of the gentry class, and the Haskells were laborers. So far, though, Haskell had not set a wrong foot forward, and he'd earned the respect of local landholders and the men he managed.

She put that worry and her own husband-hunting aside though. Helena's time was drawing near. The work needed to be done, and if they had to leave, they'd take the preserved fruits of the kitchen garden and orchard with them.

On the Thursday before the harvest festival, a hired chaise disgorged Mr. Jedidiah Morledge, the presumptive heir to Bicton Grange, on the doorstep. He'd come, he said, to attend the harvest festival and stay on through his dear cousin's confinement. An unpleasant man of middling years, Fleur took an instant dislike of him, and the sentiment was returned. She was all for sending him off to the Book and Bell, but Helena, perhaps wisely looking to her own future, gave him Cora's bedchamber and had Cora move in with Fleur.

Gareth had called only once while she'd been off running errands. Thereafter, she hadn't heard from him. Perhaps he was busy helping with the harvest at Sherington Manor.

ON THE FRIDAY BEFORE THE FESTIVAL, MRS. Knollwood waylaid Fleur in the still room, begging her to visit Mr. Clark's Mercantile for lemons they'd need for the new mother's caudle.

She was approaching the turnoff to Sherington Manor when she saw a man running toward her.

Fear made her clutch the lines, slowing the gig, and then she realized it was Haskell. Movement behind her and to her left caught her eye. In the field to the south, men were gathered around something.

The crowd shifted and she spotted a man stretched on the ground. She stopped the gig and jumped out.

One of the field workers waved. Fleur clutched her skirts and dodged through a clump of low hedging, with Haskell an arm's length behind her.

* * *

GARETH POKED HIS HEAD INTO THE STUDY AND FOUND Mr. Sherington pouring over his harvest reports.

"All's well in those last fields, sir." He handed over a written report. "Your tenants there have finished."

"I thank you, Ardleigh."

"How goes the rest?"

"I wish I knew. Where is Chigwell? He promised to report to me an hour ago."

"Not in his office. I stopped there first." He'd scraped the mud off his boots and dusted his buckskin pants before making his way deeper into the house. "Shall I go look for him?"

A few minutes later he was mounted and making

his way down the drive. At the turn onto the lane, his heart thudded.

Men were huddled in a nearby field. The Bicton-Grange cart—Fleur's cart—was stopped on the roadside. She was running—toward Sherington Manor, with a man chasing her.

His blood pounded and he spurred his horse. Even at this distance he recognized Haskell.

The devil. She ought to be shouting. Why weren't the others running to help her? Unless Haskell was chasing her toward them.

He'd break every bone in the bastard's body.

Before Gareth could reach her and scoop her up, she swerved and ran towards the group in the field.

The men parted, waved, shouted.

Gareth reined up, leapt from his mount, and hurried to join them. The bulky body, the shaggy white hair—it was Chigwell.

CHAPTER EIGHT

*S*ometime later, he found Fleur in the steward's cottage kitchen heating water for tea; a fresh pot, it seemed as Haskell was seated at the plain deal table drinking a cup, his gaze following Fleur's every move.

Outrage rose again in him, the same anger that had roared to life when he thought Haskell was chasing her.

When he stepped into the room, both Haskell and Fleur turned his way. He exchanged nods with Haskell and glared at Fleur.

She shouldn't be alone with this rough fellow.

"Doctor Wagner is with him," she said in a distant, flat voice. "You've informed Mr. Sherington?"

They'd found Chigwell conscious and breathing, but too weak to walk. While Gareth fetched the doctor, the men loaded the steward into Fleur's cart and moved him home.

"Yes," Gareth said. "He came back with me. He's just gone up to the bedchamber."

The kitchen was surprisingly modern, fitted out with a Rumsford stove. In fact, the cottage was larger than what he'd expected, with a hectare of land for a large garden and grazing.

It would indeed be a good situation for a man such as himself. If only Cheshire had the climate for grapes.

Fleur's arm wobbled hefting the steaming pot. "Let me." Haskell jumped from his chair and touched her arm, nudging her away from the stove.

It ought to have been him helping her, not this fellow. He himself had hefted many a pot around a campfire or in the mess, whereas Fleur... French, English, what did it matter? She was a lady.

Eyes blazing, her gaze met his. He pulled out a chair and settled in for a cup of hot tea. Let her be angry. He wasn't leaving.

* * *

"AND THIS WOMAN, SHE WILL BE AT THIS FÊTE?"

Marceau stood preening at the mirror in his inn room and applying a noxious scent. Having fallen in with the right crowd, his negotiations in London had gone well and he was thinking of himself as very much the bon vivant.

On the other hand, his journey to the English countryside by public coach had not been so pleasant, and when he arrived late that afternoon in Reabridge, the innkeeper at the Book and Bell had looked askance at renting a room to a Frenchman. But a bottle of decent champagne and Gareth's appearance in his regimentals to vouch for him had moved the man.

"Will she be there?" Marceau repeated.

He hoped so. He hadn't seen her since Chigwell's spell on Friday. The Sherington steward had succumbed to exhaustion, but with Haskell and Gareth supplying information, Mr. Sherington was able to tally up his year's harvest, and it had been a good one.

On Saturday, Gareth encountered the doctor coming from Bicton Grange and stopped him for news. Mrs. Bicton-Morledge was having pains; the baby might come tomorrow, or it might be several more days of misery.

Fleur might not attend the festival if she was needed at home. "If Miss Hardouin doesn't appear," Gareth said, "We shall go to her. She has agreed to meet you."

"And to marry me?" Marceau asked, watching himself in the mirror as he adjusted his neckcloth.

Irritating, pompous, jackanapes frog. "You want me to do your wooing for you?" Gareth asked.

Marceau turned abruptly from the mirror, his dark eyes flashing. "Is *that* what you've been doing? Why you didn't write when you first discovered her? Do not tell me you got to her first."

Gareth tossed the other man's hat, hitting him squarely in the chest, wishing it had been his fist. "She is a lady, and you will speak of her with respect."

The Frenchman shrugged.

"And while we're discussing respect, Marceau, you must be on your best behavior." They'd been speaking in French, and Gareth switched to English. "You're a Frenchman, visiting a village filled with veterans of Waterloo and all the battles that came before, and many villagers whose sons will never come home."

"Bah, *oui*, Anglais. You are right. Eh, the coach ride, it was all evil eyes." His lips firmed and his eyes narrowed. "And here, you, you will... will guard me as I guarded you. You have a debt to me, *n'est pas*, and to the Veuve." He wrinkled his nose. "Tell me at least, is she pretty?"

Too pretty for you. He walked out of the room and headed for the brisk air of the innyard, scented as it was with horses and the smoke from the landlord's kitchen fire, smells he preferred over Etienne's eau de cologne.

. . .

GARETH WASN'T THE ONLY MAN SPORTING A UNIFORM this day. There were men decked out in the blue coats of the Cheshire militia, some in the green tunics of the Rifles, and others in the red with varying colors of sashes. Reabridge and environs had stood stoutly for king and country. Marceau had best mind his Ps and Qs this day.

He saw the housekeeper from Bicton Grange bending over the wares in a stall laden with colorful beads. Telling Marceau to wait, Gareth stalked over to speak to her.

"Ma'am." He lifted his hat. "Is Miss Hardouin here today?"

"She's gone to the dressing tent to help mend a costume." She pointed to a closed pavilion on the edge of the green. "If you go that way, tell her I'll be right along. We've got to get back to Bicton Grange and relieve Cora. Her ma insists Cora will have some fun tonight at the ball."

"Fleur won't be there?"

The housekeeper shook her head. "Lady Ixton will chaperone Cora. With her time this close, we won't leave the mistress with just the maids."

Gareth had best hurry then. Excusing himself, he walked that way, beckoning Marceau.

He ducked his head under the turned-up flap and stifled an oath.

Costumes cluttered one table, and another held threads and sewing implements. Fleur's back was turned, and she was not alone.

Haskell saw him first. The ass was decked out in a crown woven from barley and a mantle embroidered with tufts of various grains. In his hand, he held a scythe swathed in ribbons.

"Hold still." Fleur tied off a thread and snipped it. "There. Your wheat will stay in place, your majesty."

In the far corner, a woman giggled. She held a baby and was doing up the ties on her gown, as if she'd just taken it off the tit.

"Don't let it go to your head, Bevan Haskell," the woman said.

Gareth cleared his throat and Fleur whipped around. A work smock covered her plain lavender gown, but lovely golden tendrils had escaped her bonnet, kissing her forehead and cheeks. Her gaze shifted ever so slightly to the man appearing next to him, and the color that had pinkened her cheeks drained away.

Her stillness, her stoic mask, tore at his guts. But they must go on.

Gareth nodded to the Lord of the Harvest and the woman. "Haskell," he said, "a moment with Miss Hardouin if you please?"

Fleur nodded.

"I'll be right outside." Haskell's proprietary glance

raised Gareth's hackles. Lord of the Harvest or not, the upstart had no claim on Fleur.

"You remember my sister, Sadie?" Haskell said.

He'd had a moment's thought that this was Haskell's woman and child, but his cringing sister? Gareth inclined his head as they passed, exchanging parting glares with Haskell.

When he turned back to Fleur, she'd frozen, a pair of scissors poised like a weapon.

"Shall I take those?" She surrendered them without resistance, and the chill of her hands made him want to grasp them and warm them. Instead, he set his hand to the small of her stiff back. "Miss Hardouin," he said. "May I introduce to you Etienne Marceau?"

As he watched, her lips sealed together in a tight line. Still, he must soldier on.

"Etienne Marceau," Gareth said, "Miss Fleur Hardouin."

To his credit, Marceau gave a courtly bow. Fleur inclined her head a fraction like a duchess meeting the lowliest of courtiers.

Her color was coming back, and his heart lifted. Whether she married Marceau or not, the Frenchman was part of her family. At least Gareth had managed to give her that.

"My dear cousin." Marceau moved closer, and Fleur's eyebrows rose a fraction. "We have found you after so many years. Captain Ardleigh didn't tell me how beautiful you are."

Marceau did look stunned. If he was feigning interest, he was doing an admirable job of it.

"I must speak to you about a delicate matter. Perhaps in private?"

She raised one shoulder in a shrug. "I don't know you. Captain Ardleigh will stay."

Irritation flashed across the younger man's face. "But of course. We don't know each other. But I have traveled all the way from France to bring you this news that your family wishes you to return. It is your grandmother's most fervent, er, desire that you and I, we join our families more closely together."

He paused for a breath. Fleur blinked.

"I am of the family Marceau and you of the Hardouins, and together, Hardouin-Marceau, we are makers of the finest sparkling wine in all of Champagne. I am to bring you to France to meet the Veuve Hardouin, and there, my dear, we will be married."

After his pause for breath, Marceau had switched to French.

"Marceau," Gareth said, gently, in English, "Miss Hardouin, doesn't speak French."

Marceau's eyes widened. "A Frenchwoman who does not speak French?"

"I am not French," Fleur said. "I am English. It is my most fervent desire to stay in England."

"I like England," Marceau said, nodding. "London, to be precise. And it is my hope to spend much time here about the business. I shall arrange a house for us there."

"Arrange a house for yourself then. I will not marry you, sir."

FLEUR HELD HER BREATH, WATCHING THE PLAY OF emotions across young Etienne Marceau's handsome face. He was indeed young, and though his coat was a sober blue, and his buckskin trousers were fashionably tight, his waistcoat sported bright red flowers with curling vines on a primrose field, and his starched white neckcloth had been tied up to his ears in an intricate knot and pierced with a red-jeweled stickpin. His dark good looks would turn heads among the ladies of Reabridge.

Not her head though. The younger man paled next to Gareth Ardleigh who was a picture of virile masculinity. Selfish, scheming, virile masculinity, perhaps, but the arrogance had been tempered by something special in him.

Had always been.

"But you must marry me," the young Frenchman said. He turned to Gareth. "Tell her she must. It is all arranged," he said in French. "Why did you not write me? Are you sure this is the right woman? Why, her mother's grandfather was a chevalier, and look at her, a colorless drab; why, even the modistes of London dress better."

Fleur's hands curled into fists and her pulse pounded in her ears as the words rolled over and through her and overwhelmed her.

She didn't, couldn't *speak* French, but she'd understood all of that.

"That's enough," Gareth growled.

Still, the Frenchman's tantrum raged on. "No polite greeting, no smiles, no femininity." He paced and pounded a table sending the needles, spools, and scissors jumping. His eyes bulged and a vein throbbed in his forehead. "*Mon Dieu.*" His fingers launched his carefully arranged curls in all directions. He was much like the youngest Bicton-Morledge girl when she was in a nursery room snit.

Fleur smothered a chuckle with her hand and backed away.

"You," the Frenchman said, poking his finger in Gareth's chest. "You deceived me, me, who saved your life. You present me with this, this drab, this milkmaid, this—"

Gareth's fist flew with a powerful crack and the Frenchman lurched backward knocking over a chair. "You will cease insulting Fleur, here and now," he shouted.

The Frenchman bounced up, and punches flew back and forth, some landing with sickening thuds.

Blood trickled from the Frenchman's nose and the corner of Gareth's mouth.

Haskell appeared at the tent's entrance, a Morris man poking in next to him. Fleur skirted the fight, edging toward the exit.

"Fleur is beautiful." Gareth punched. "Kind." He struck again. "And wise."

The younger man blocked the next punch and landed a blow that struck Gareth's shoulder, sending him staggering back, gasping.

His shoulder. Was that where he'd been wounded? If so, it was a low blow by a man who would have known of the wound. Fleur took a step closer and stopped.

Eyes wide, the Frenchman advanced. "I'm...I'm sorry," he said. "But—stop hitting me, Ardleigh."

Fleur touched Gareth's elbow. "Your shoulder?"

He glanced at her, dazed.

"Will you want the constable?" the Morris man asked.

"Don't be daft. It's a gentlemen's dispute." Haskell nudged the other man out of the tent.

Gareth nodded, and something passed between Haskell and Gareth.

"All settled?" Gareth quirked a bleeding eyebrow at the Frenchman. "Yes?"

"*Oui.*" He nodded. "Yes. A thousand pardons, Miss Hardouin. It is a relief that you didn't understand."

Gareth turned and looked down at her. "Oh, but you did understand, didn't you, Fleur?"

Heart pounding, insides shaking, she struggled for a breath to speak. No one else but Dulcinea knew her so well.

"You're bleeding," she finally managed to say. She lifted a corner of her shawl, but he covered her hand with his.

"Wait." He reached into a pocket and dug out a large square of cloth. "Use this."

It was no more than a rag, sporting stains and holes here and there. And a border of yellow flowers, some of them partially unraveled.

"My lady's colors," he said. "My lucky talisman."

That summer's day flashed in her memory, and she saw the young Gareth, laughing at her pathetic attempt at needlework. Since then she'd improved, imagining she was just as skilled as her mother had been.

Thoughts of her mother brought more memories: a doll with stitched gray eyes, flaxen silk hair, and a gown embroidered with flowers and bees. Lost, somewhere, in a dark place.

The stitching blurred. The beautiful man before her blurred. She crumpled the cloth in her hand, and her breath came in short, panicked gasps and she backed to the door.

"Miss Hardouin." Mrs. Knollwood was at her elbow. "The dancing starts soon, Miss Cora—"

"Yes, yes." She had duties.

She dabbed at her eyes with the cloth, and then handed it back to Gareth. "Use this for the blood. I must go. Helena needs me. Cora must go to the ball."

* * *

GARETH HELD THE CLOTH STILL DAMP FROM HER tears and swiped at a drip of blood. Wide-eyed and vulnerable, Fleur looked stunned behind a misting of tears. Fleur was crying. His Fleur.

Haskell hovered nearby. Oh yes, Cora must come and dance with the King of the Harvest.

To hell with that.

She slipped off her smock and handed it to the housekeeper.

"Fleur, wait." Gareth grabbed her free elbow. "Not yet. Don't leave yet."

She shook her head. Tears glistened on her cheeks.

"I…" The words stuck. He cleared his dry throat, swallowed, and tried again. "I love you, Petal."

Astonishment lit her face, and his confidence rose.

"Marry me," he said.

Her labored breath sent her chest rising and falling and he remembered the swell of her breasts in the yellow gown she'd worn to dinner at

Sherington Manor, and the taste of the lips she was biting.

Her eyes fluttered closed a moment, and she shook her head. "Not now. I must go."

"Wait, Fleur."

But she was already gone, and Haskell had left with her.

He hurried out of the tent, prepared to chase her, but a hand gripping his arm tugged him back, wrenching his sore shoulder again.

Gareth turned in anger.

"Sorry," Marceau said, holding up his hands. "Sorry. But don't run after her, my friend. Not yet."

SOME MINUTES LATER, GARETH FOUND HIMSELF IN the tap room of the Book and Bell. Too numb to fight more, he'd allowed himself to be dragged off by the impertinent Frenchman, who'd pushed him onto a bench and set a pint and a bottle before him. Having noticed the curious looks from other patrons, Marceau kept his voice low and spoke carefully in English.

"I would have brought champagne with me to your village," he said, "had I known we would both be made fools of by that chit of a woman."

Gareth glared at the Frenchman and started to rise. "No, no," Marceau said. "You've beat on me enough today. I apologize again. She's not a chit—

whatever that word means. She's… cold; stubborn, and, and… hard. She reminds me of the Veuve."

Gareth tossed back his brandy and poured some more. Had he not made that comparison himself before?

But Marceau was wrong. Fleur wasn't cold. One only had to look at her determination to take care of Lady Ixworth and the Bicton-Morledge females.

"You don't know anything," he said.

"No?" Marceau shrugged. "I made an offer of marriage and was refused. My pride, it was crushed. I've never offered marriage before, though Marie has hinted at it often enough."

Rightly so. She'd borne his child, and Marceau in his own selfish way, cared for the girl. Gareth didn't hold with the notion of men keeping more than one household.

"But then I see her tell you no, and me, I feel better," Marceau said.

"Shut up," Gareth said.

"I say to myself, ha, not only a marriage offer, but a declaration of love. And the girl, she cries. She loves you too."

"She doesn't love me."

"No? What was that rag you handed her? Her heart, it was in her eyes when she saw it."

Was it? All he remembered was her tears. Tears. From his Petal. What was he to do?

"I had no notion you were so… so… I say to

myself, c'est un véritable romantique. I should have known, eh bien, the way you... you whipped the Veuve around your small finger. You've done the same to the granddaughter."

Gareth drained his glass again, letting Marceau babble on.

"Tonight, my friend, you get drunk. Tomorrow, we shall go visit my cousin again."

Gareth reached for the bottle, but Marceau pulled it away from him. "But first, before you are too... too... How do you say it, bosky? First, we must make a plan for how you will win the hand of your lady and whip the Veuve again around all of your fingers and your whole hand."

CHAPTER NINE

"It's the whole bloody business of war," Gareth said. He'd listened to a litany of bad memories, and now it was his turn to speak.

His head pounded like the devil and the breakfast Marceau forced on him threatened to come up. He was damnably hungover, and this hastily assembled meeting of Reabridge veterans at Doctor Wagner's surgery wasn't helping his disposition. "We do our duty," he said, "they do theirs, and in the midst of all the dutiful are the madmen who enjoy it." He'd seen that in the eyes of all stripes—French, English, and Spaniards; men and women; soldiers and civilians. "Not that I don't enjoy a good fight, God knows, but..." He took in a breath. "Not just what they did to us, or what we did to them, but what they did to each other." What they'd done to Fleur, who like other children bore the wounds of abandonment.

He rubbed his scraggly jaw. Marceau's razor had been dull by the time he'd borrowed it. "I'm not making sense I guess, but when I close my eyes I see that last battle and what came after..."

He straightened and prayed that this damn meeting would end soon. Pain settled about the men and one woman gathered there, as thick and stifling as the smoke they'd all fought through in Flanders and every other bloody battlefield.

Still, discipline held as they listened to stories, all different and yet the same.

Finally a desperate knocking at the door brought a pause. Dr. Wagner went to the door, spoke to someone, and turned back to the room.

"I must go deliver a baby," he said.

Gareth stood. "Whose?"

Wagner gave him a long look.

"Is it Mrs. Bicton-Morledge?" Gareth asked.

Wagner nodded.

"I'm coming with you."

GARETH ARRIVED AT BICTON GRANGE TO FIND George Sherington on the doorstep. The maid greeting them said the doctor was upstairs with the ladies of the house, the little girls were in the nursery under Cora's care, the footman had gone for the family's solicitor, and Mr. Morledge was in the parlor.

They were in for a long afternoon, and Gareth offered to check on the Morledge girls in the nursery and fetch tea. When he returned with a tray, he found Sherington deep in conversation with a stout man, dressed all in black, as if attending a wake. So this was Morledge.

"About time," Morledge said. "I've pulled the bell three times. Who are you, and why don't you have a decent shave?"

"Captain Gareth Ardleigh," Sherington said, "Meet Mr. Jedidiah Morledge. And thank you for doing footman work."

"All in the name of duty," Gareth said. He sent Morledge a terse nod. "There's a baby being born here; the staff is busy with more important things than your bell-tugging."

"Are the girls well?" Sherington asked.

"Yes. Cora enjoyed the harvest ball last night."

Morledge harrumphed. "Made a spectacle of herself with that bumpkin, the Lord of the Harvest."

Gareth straightened to his full height, six inches taller than the other man. "How so?" he asked.

"Danced with the fellow twice. A common laborer."

"A common laborer who might find himself a job as a land steward soon. Lady Ixworth and I were there," Sherington said. "There was nothing untoward about it." He poured his own tea and looked up. "Very kind of Miss Hardouin to spend the evening with Helena so Cora could attend."

She'd been needed here. How could he fault her for not staying to speak with him?

Hope rose in him. He would try again, soon, after this baby was born.

Turning, he paced to the window. But if it was a girl, what were they to do? He couldn't in good conscience promise to provide for all of them. Perhaps if he took Sherington's offer they could all live at the Manor. He'd have to give up his dreams of vineyards, but he'd have Fleur. Dear Fleur.

But... what had Sherington said about a land steward? Was he thinking of hiring Haskell if Gareth didn't want the position?

Oh hell. That would set Haskell up well to marry Cora. How could he interfere with their happiness?

"Tea's too strong," Morledge complained. "What kind of staff does Helena employ?"

He itched to snatch the fellow up by his neck cloth. "I made the tea." Gareth came and loomed over the oaf's chair. "It's just like the tea we served in the officer's mess. I say, Morledge, why are you here, anyway?"

Morledge spluttered into his cup, grabbed a napkin and wiped at his mouth.

"Damned nuisance for the family having you lurking about, waiting for this babe. Your presence won't make a damn bit of difference."

Sherington nodded and sat back in chair, steepling his fingers and watching the other man stutter for words.

"Are we in some medieval mystery play?" Gareth said. "Are we worried someone will slip in a male child? A peasant boy to take the king's crown?"

"I don't have to answer to you. Why the devil are you here, Captain?"

"Friend of the family," Gareth said.

"Well, I *am* family. I'm the heir. *And I want you gone.*"

"No. Captain Ardleigh is here at my request." Sherington's tone was affable. "If you'll remember, Morledge, I'm both the Justice of the Peace and a guardian to Bicton-Morledge's children. Captain Ardleigh will stay."

"Now see here, Sherington. You threw me out once—"

"And I'll do it again."

A tap came at the parlor door. Haskell's muscular bulk was framed in the doorway.

Gareth was glad to see him. Haskell had no cause to be an ally of Morledge. *The enemy of my enemy is my friend.*

"Ah, Haskell," Sherington said. "Come in."

"We didn't hear the door knocker," Morledge said.

"We came in through the kitchens." Haskell stepped aside, and Gareth recognized the woman from the tent, Haskell's sister with the same sleeping baby, a child several months old.

"Sadie," Sherington said, "did they send for you already?"

"Yes sir," she said, bobbing a curtsey. "Reckon it will be soon."

"What's this?" Morledge stood. "You make jokes about substituting a male child, and see what we have here—"

"This here's my baby girl." Sadie lifted her chubby chin. "Any soul with a brain knows a ten-month-old from a newborn."

Gareth bit down on a grin.

While Sherington made introductions, Gareth picked up the tea tray. "I'll just replenish these and maybe there'll be news."

He stalked out and was surprised to find Haskell following.

"What news?" Haskell asked.

"Nothing so far. The doctor and the ladies are with her. I passed that floor on my way to the nursery and heard a great deal of groaning. Cora has the girls well in hand. I suppose it wouldn't go amiss for you to visit the nursery and check on them."

Haskell sent him a puzzled look.

"That ass is just biding his time to put them all out of the house," Gareth said. "I hope you're not planning to leave. Am I correct that your sister is here to help with the, er, feeding?"

"Yes." Haskell nodded.

"I'll fetch a whole plate of tarts for her."

Haskell nodded again. "Thank you. I'll check on the little ones, and then after Sadie is fed, we'll send her up to see what's what."

"A good plan."

They parted ways. He was in the kitchen putting the final touches to his tray when the housekeeper herself rushed in, tears streaming.

His heart dropped into his stomach as the older woman threw herself into his arms. "Oh, Captain." She stepped away, breathless. "Oh Captain. It's a *boy*. And the doctor says there's another babe crowning. I must have the caudle, Cook. And more hot water. And clean linens. Send whoever you can find to the linen closet."

She grabbed a steaming pitcher and rushed out again.

On his way up the stairs with the burden of tea and cakes, a noise like a cat crying filtered down from above.

* * *

FLEUR WIPED TEARS ON HER SLEEVE AND HELD Helena's hand and her own breath as with one final straining push, the second baby arrived.

She'd never witnessed childbirth before. Helena's bravery was astonishing.

"Another boy." Dr. Wagner grinned and handed the wailing babe off to Miss Barlow. Mrs. Knollwood set the first babe to Helena's breast, and his crying stopped.

"A boy," Helena said.

"Two boys." Dulcinea mopped the exhausted lady's forehead with a dampened towel. "And Miss Barlow has tied a ribbon around the heir's foot."

"Indeed I did." Miss Barlow said, gently cleaning the second babe. "We'll know better soon, but I don't think they're identical."

"We've one more task here, Helena," Dr. Wagner said. "Let's get all of that afterbirth out."

A short time later, Fleur was taking away soiled linens when Haskell's sister Sadie entered the room, a baby in her arms.

"Two boys," Fleur said.

Sadie grinned. "*Two?* That Morledge will be fit to be tied. When Captain Ardleigh came up from the kitchen—"

"Captain Ardleigh is here?"

"Aye, and with Mr. Sherington. Bevan too."

Her heart did a flip and she was suddenly nervous. *Gareth was here.*

"Fleur, go tell the gentlemen the good news," Dulcinea called. "I'll be right along to do battle with Mr. Morledge."

"You won't have to," Sadie said. "My brother and the captain are up to the task."

Fleur took off her soiled smock, smoothed her hair, and made herself walk sedately down the stairs, though her insides were quaking.

Watching Helena's struggles made her realize she'd been taking the coward's way out. Gareth was right: she needed to visit this woman who claimed to be her grandmother.

And, oh, if he would have her, if he would ask her again, there was no one better than Gareth to journey with.

When she entered the parlor, the heated conversation in progress halted.

Morledge stood, looking trapped between Haskell and Gareth. Mr. Sherington pushed himself to his feet.

"The crying has stopped," Morledge said. "Is the child still alive?"

Fleur gasped. "Indeed, he is, Mr. Morledge. And so is his little brother. Helena has delivered twin boys."

The color drained from Morledge's face and then rose again in a flare of anger. "Gloat if you will, but many infants die unexpectedly."

Gareth gripped his arm. "Are you threatening murder?"

Morledge tried to pull away. "I'm saying what's true. Why, a careless nursemaid, a fall down the stairs, a passing fever—"

"Morledge," Mr. Sherington said. "I caution you

to stop speaking. There are four witnesses here. If something should happen to either lad, some accident, why, you have motive, and you are discussing means."

"It's too unbelievable. After a passel of girls, she has two boys? I would see these babies."

"It's best if you would leave," Sherington said.

Morledge stuttered a protest. Gareth and Haskell exchanged a look, Mr. Sherington nodded, and Fleur scurried out of the way as the men grabbed the villain's elbows, carted him to the front door, and all but tossed him out.

They were dusting their hands and grinning like two schoolboys when the knocker sounded again. Gareth's frowned and yanked open the door.

Etienne Marceau stumbled in. "I say." He glanced over his shoulder. Morledge was climbing into a cart. "That's my cart," Marceau called.

"Let him go," Gareth said. "We've just tossed him out."

Marceau frowned. "Bad news, my friend?"

Gareth clapped him on the back and laughed. "The lady of the house has just had twin boys. Fleur, may we make your cousin welcome?"

She threw up her hands. "Why not? Make introductions and I'll go find some brandy."

"But look," Marceau said, drawing a bottle out of the pocket of his great coat. "I have brought champagne."

Gareth exchanged a look with the Frenchman and then crossed the room to take her hands.

"Brandy would be welcome as well. If you please, Fleur, tell me where it is, and I'll fetch it."

The tenderness in his voice rendered her speechless. She shook her head and pulled her hands free.

As she hurried away, she heard Gareth whisper, "We haven't got that far yet. Fleur has been busy."

He'd spoken in French.

She sniffed, swiped at a tear, and made her way to the butler's pantry.

BY THE TIME SHE RETURNED TO THE PARLOR, SHE'D composed herself. Dulcinea had joined Sherington on the sofa. Haskell and Marceau stood eyeing each other warily.

Gareth hurried over, took the tray with the bottle and glasses and set it aside.

He grasped her hands and dropped to one knee, and her heart froze. Before she could summon her brain, he spoke.

"I won't wait another moment, Fleur." He spoke loudly enough to be heard in the next county. "I love you. Would you make me the happiest of men? Would you do me the honor of becoming my wife?"

She heard her own shallow breath, and the

ticking of a clock, and the rustling of footsteps somewhere in the house.

Gareth's gaze held steady on hers, perspiration beading on his forehead and trickling down to his jaw.

"Have you your handkerchief?" she asked.

He blinked, and his lips turned up. The corner of his mouth had scabbed from his fight yesterday. She wondered if it would bleed again if she kissed him.

Gareth freed a hand, reached into his pocket, and placed a cloth in her hand. The same one.

"I carried it all through the Peninsula. Took it to Flanders. I didn't have it with me when I was captured."

Her vision blurred as she dabbed at his face. "I must make you a new one."

He jumped to his feet. "You haven't said yes, but don't say no yet. I don't have much, but I have prospects."

She raised up on her toes, leaned close to his ear, and whispered. "And you have me."

"For heaven's sake, Fleur," Dulcinea said.

"Now, now," Sherington said. "While you're deciding, Dulcy and I have an announcement. "We are to marry. You will always have a home with us, Fleur. Unless you decide to make other arrangements. I understand that Mssr. Marceau's great aunt wishes you to marry him."

Gareth's arm tightened around her. "She won't

marry him. She's going to marry me." He grinned down at her. "Yes?" All of his great heart shone in his eyes.

"Yes," she nodded. "Yes, I will. And I think... I think we must visit Champagne. I think your enthusiasm for wine must be pursued."

"Bien," Marceau said. "At last. You see, Ardleigh, the Hardouin blood runs true. You will not regret it, cousin, and you will be much happier married to Ardleigh than to me."

* * *

A FEW WEEKS LATER.

THE HIGHEST AND LOWEST FAMILIES FILLED THE PEWS of St. Beonna's for the double wedding of two joyful couples. The joint wedding breakfast took place at Bicton Grange, after which George Sherington carried his new bride off to Sherington Manor.

But Fleur and Gareth would spend their wedding night in a cottage on the grounds, one hastily spruced up for the newlyweds. The larder had been filled, but they would otherwise have to do for themselves, which suited them just fine.

When they arrived, Gareth swept her up and carried her across the threshold, and then into the bedchamber with its tester bed and new mattress.

Covered plates sat next to a bottle of champagne—vin de comete--nestled in ice. The bedding had been turned back and a nightgown laid out.

Gareth settled his arm around her. "Shall we turn in early?" he teased.

"I see my nightgown. I'm wondering where is your night shirt?"

His low chuckle tickled her ear. Moments later his lips followed, moving from her ear down to the place below it, sending shivers through her.

She turned in his arms and linked her hands behind his head. "Dulcinea thought it necessary to explain the wedding night to me."

"I would have loved to have heard that lecture." He swept one finger along her jawline, past the pulse in her neck, and along the edge of her decolletage. Pleasure pulsed along the places he touched.

"As if after years of her sly innuendos, not to mention living on an estate where animals were bred, I wouldn't already have a somewhat clear idea of matters. I just never quite understood why the eagerness to engage."

Gareth blinked and then a slow smile formed. "You, puss, are challenging me."

"Am I?" She grinned, and then laughed, and when he slipped his hand under her bodice, she gasped and surrendered.

EPILOGUE

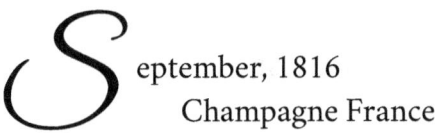eptember, 1816
Champagne France

FLEUR TUCKED UP HER BODICE AND HANDED HER bundled lass to the older lady, who clucked and patted and dropped kisses on the forehead of the gurgling baby before setting her to her shoulder.

"She'll spit up on you, madame," Gareth said, pulling Fleur out of her chair.

The Veuve sent them both a crinkly smile. "Enjoy the moonlight, while I sing this little one to sleep." She set off for the house, already crooning off-key.

"Walk with me," he said. "Under the harvest moon."

She glanced up at the clear night sky and pulled her shawl tighter. Just one year ago, on a night like this, he'd asked her to marry him, and she'd run away.

When she shivered, he tugged her against him, putting his arms around her. The scents of starch and the musk of hard work and virile manhood filled her as the warmth of him seeped into her. She rubbed her cheek against his linen shirt and turned her lips up for a quick kiss that tasted like sweet champagne.

"This moment." He sighed. "Ah heaven. A good harvest. Good champagne. A magical full moon."

She smiled up at him. "A Champagne moon."

"Yes." He leaned in and she lifted her chin expecting another kiss.

But he stopped, and his rumbling murmur made her quiver. "Who would have thought it? You, my beautiful woman, and me, under the Champagne moon."

With a laugh, she pulled him down for a kiss that went on, and on, and on.

THE END

AFTERWORD

I hope you've enjoyed reading Gareth's and Fleur's story as much as I did writing it.

The idea for Fleur's background came to me when I was taking an online class offered by the Regency Fiction Writers group. The topic was "The Gentleman's Drink" and one of the Regency era beverages covered was champagne. We learned about the Veuve Clicquot, a widow who persuaded her father-in-law to let her take over the running of the winery during the Napoleonic era in France. Her innovations spurred the development of champagne, and the Veuve Clicquot brand still prospers today. In fact, I just saw it for sale among the premium brands at our neighborhood Costco!

I've taken the liberty of making Fleur's grandmother much older than the real Veuve, who was only thirty-eight in 1815. My story, and all of the characters in it, are of course entirely fictional.

This story first appeared in *Under the Harvest Moon, a Bluestocking Belles with Friends Collection*. Many thanks go to the participating Belles, Jude Knight, Rue Allyn, Cerise DeLand, Caroline Warfield, Elizabeth Ellen Carter and Sherry Ewing, as well as friends Collette Cameron and Mary Lancaster. The collection was a group effort of beta reading, and the insights of such skilled and experienced writers were invaluable. Special thanks go to the final editor, Jude Knight.

If you have time and you're so inclined, please consider leaving a review at the bookseller of your choice. I would be immensely grateful!

BOOKS BY ALINA K. FIELD

SONS OF THE SPY LORD SERIES

MARRYING MR. GIBSON

Previously titled *The Bastard's Iberian Bride*

Paulette Heardwyn rushes to visit her dying guardian, set on learning the truth about her father. But the only man with answers takes his secrets to the grave, leaving her penniless—unless she marries his illegitimate son.

https://alinakfield.com/book/marrying-mr-gibson/

THE VISCOUNT'S SEDUCTION

Lady Sirena Hollister has lost everything, even her fey abilities. But when the fairies hand her a chance at a London Season, her schemes for revenge stir up an unknown enemy, and spark danger of a different sort, in the person of a handsome Viscount.

https://alinakfield.com/book/the-viscounts-seduction/

THE ROGUE'S LAST SCANDAL

Falling—literally—into the arms of the *ton*'s most

outrageous rogue seems a risky path of escape, but Maria
Graciela Kingsley y Romero has no other choice. Only
England's greatest spy lord can help her, and he is not to
be found—so his son will have to do!

https://alinakfield.com/book/rogues-last-scandal/

THE COUNTERFEIT LADY

Vowing she'll never submit to an arranged marriage, an
earl's daughter bolts for the seaside cottage that will
someday be hers. But she finds her quiet refuge occupied
by the last man she ever wants to see—an American artist,
who's also a thief. And quite possibly one of her father's
spies.

https://alinakfield.com/book/the-counterfeit-lady/

AVENGING THE EARL'S LADY

The long war is over, but honor requires vanquishing one
last enemy, and the Earl of Shaldon has no time for
romance. But when the lady he longs for interferes in his
plot, and his enemy strikes at her, nothing else matters
but avenging his lady.

https://alinakfield.com/book/avenging-the-earls-lady/

NOVELLAS AND HOLIDAY STORIES: THE MARQUESS AND THE MIDWIFE

Finalist, 2016 National Reader's Choice Award

Uncovering a lie drives a new marquess back from a self-imposed exile at Christmas to find the only woman he's ever loved. Finding her turns out to be easy, uncovering her stunning secrets, a bit harder. But winning her back will be the greatest challenge of all.

https://alinakfield.com/book/the-marquess-and-the-midwife/

A LEAP INTO LOVE

Can a gentleman be too charming?

The ladies of Upper Upton think so.

When the single ladies of the village conspire to teach their charmer a lesson that might bankrupt him, the town's loveliest young widow—who's sworn off marriage forever—steps up to warn him.

https://alinakfield.com/book/a-leap-into-love/

LILIANA'S LETTER: FINALIST, 2015 NATIONAL READER'S CHOICE AWARD

The Matchmaker Meets the Matchbreaker

Liliana Ashford's future as a professional chaperone depends on her wealthy charge's successful marriage, but her own close encounter with a scoundrel years ago makes her determined to save the girl from the same kind of rogue.

https://alinakfield.com/book/lilianas-letter/

THE GHOST OF DEPFORD HALL

A sweet Halloween short story

It's her mother's last All Hallows' Eve.

When family, friends, and tenants gather, goblins, ghouls, and ghosts are banned from this All Hallows' Eve party.

Only, no one told the Ghost of Depford Hall!

https://alinakfield.com/book/ghost-depford-hall/

COURTED BY THE EARL

Previously titled Bella's Band

A 2015 RONE Award Finalist

Saddled with his brother's title and debts, nothing about this new life makes the Earl of Hackwell want to stay—until he meets a lady with a secret that can change everything.

https://alinakfield.com/book/courted-by-the-earl/

ROSALYN'S RING: 2014 BOOK BUYER'S BEST WINNER, NOVELLA CATEGORY

Done with grieving her losses, a late nobleman's daughter has fallen into a tidy spinster's life in London. But when one snowy Christmas Eve, a young woman needs rescue, she seizes the chance to do good—and to recover a family heirloom that ought to be hers.

https://alinakfield.com/book/rosalyns-ring/

HAUNTING MISS FENWICK

Thrilled to finally have a permanent home, a Squire's daughter won't let a supernatural creature scare her away. While hunting the ghost she doesn't believe in, she stumbles upon a mysterious flesh and blood man who might be the key to all of her problems.

https://alinakfield.com/book/haunting-miss-fenwick/

LADY TWISDEN'S PICTURE PERFECT MATCH

Promised York's marriage mart and the hospitality of his cousin's doddering stepmother, Major August Kellborn is shocked to find that his fetching hostess is the one woman who stirs his heart.

https://alinakfield.com/book/lady-twisdens-picture-perfect-match/

FLOWERS FOR HIS LADY

Eleanor Gurnwood has only one goal in sight: to make this year's Christmas service beautiful for the parishioners of St. Tancred's—until the Christmas eve when a man from her past rides in on a white horse.

https://alinakfield.com/book/flowers-for-his-lady/

THE UPSTART CHRISTMAS BRIDES SERIES

THE DUKE SHE DESPISED

Hiding her true identity, a young vicar's widow takes a position as housekeeper in a remote Scottish castle at Christmas for a new duke who years ago sabotaged her chance for happiness. She quickly falls for the duke's charming but not very competent factor, not knowing that he's hiding something also—he's the duke she despised!

https://alinakfield.com/book/the-duke-she-despised/

CONVINCING THE COUNTESS

A penniless widowed countess with trade in her blood descends upon the country manor of her sons' negligent guardian, intent on confronting him about her boys' futures. Instead, she finds his younger brother, a business-minded aristocrat with a penchant for widows and a distaste for emotional entanglements. A man who once witnessed her greatest humiliation. A man offering enticing distractions that threaten to derail all her plans.

https://alinakfield.com/book/convincing-the-countess/

THE IMPETUOUS HEIRESS

Before dashing Lord Loughton can make amends with his neglected fiancée, the lady's meddling cousin delivers her to his doorstep. He soon realizes more is amiss than his carelessness. Can he uncover her secrets and win her back before he loses her altogether?

https://alinakfield.com/book/the-impetuous-heiress/

THE NABOB'S DESIGNING DAUGHTER

Ripped from his prestigious London practice to deliver a Highland duke's heir, a young doctor finds there are more snares awaiting than a risky birth, including a surprise— and worthless—bequest. There's also his best friend's cousin, who's blossomed from mousey to heart-stirringly beautiful, with enough wiles to convince an ambitious man that his heart belongs in the Highlands.

https://alinakfield.com/book/the-nabobs-designing-daughter/

THE EARL'S SCOTTISH HOYDEN

Coerced by her brother to spend an English Christmas at the country estate of the handsome but cold earl who all but jilted her a year earlier, Edme Beecham is determined to do no more than assist her brother in his business negotiations with the earl, and by all means, to protect her heart.

https://alinakfield.com/book/the-earls-scottish-hoyden/

THE MACBETH SERIES

FATED HEARTS

A Love After All Retelling of the Scottish Play

A Scottish Baron returning from two decades at war meets the wife he divorced and the daughter he disavowed before she was born, only to learn that everything he'd believed was a lie. Determined to win back the only woman he's ever loved he must first face the viper who drove them apart.

https://alinakfield.com/book/fated-hearts/

THE COMTESSE OF MIDNIGHT

A Scottish Earl on a quest for the elusive Comtesse de Fontenay, rescues a French lady smuggler during a devastating storm, taking shelter with her. As the stormy night drags on, he suspects she knows the lady he's seeking, the lady who holds the secret to his identity.

https://alinakfield.com/book/the-comtesse-of-midnight/

CLAIMS OF THE HEART

Since a perilous fall, Lucie Macbeth has been seeing more than a settled future as the heiress to a Scottish barony. The visions plaguing her include a man—one far above her class and breeding, and English to boot. He's engaged to a duke's granddaughter as well, and thus wholly inappropriate. Though she can't marry him, and she won't become any man's leman, when the Sight warns her of danger to him, her conscience, and her heart tell her she can't walk away.

https://alinakfield.com/book/claims-of-the-heart/

UNDER THE HARVEST MOON

A Bluestocking Belles Collection with Friends

As the village of Reabridge in Cheshire prepares for the first Harvest Festival following Waterloo, families are overjoyed to welcome back their loved ones from the war. This collection of nine engaging tales has mysteries, secrets, tensions, reunions, romance, and makes for an unforgettable read.

Includes *Under the Champagne Moon*,

by Alina K. Field.

https://alinakfield.com/book/under-the-harvest-moon/

COMING DECEMBER 26, 2024

CHRISTMASTIDE KISSES

A Bluestocking Belles Collection with Friends

Six stories of love and romance at Christmas, includes *Twelfth Night Treasure,* by Alina K. Field, a short, sweet sequel to *Flowers for his Lady*

COMING JUNE 11, 2024:

A WALLFLOWER'S MIDSUMMER NIGHT'S CAPER

Book 15 in The Revenge of the Wallflowers multi-author collection.

A Midsummer Night's masquerade at her family's country home presents the Honorable Nancy Lovelace with the perfect opportunity for revenge against the man who ruined her first London season—a man she's known since childhood, a man she once thought she loved.

https://alinakfield.com/book/a-wallflowers-midsummer-nights-caper/